Love
Me
Tender

CATHERINE
TEXIER

PENGUIN BOOKS

PENGUIN BOOKS
Viking Penguin Inc., 40 West 23rd Street,
New York, New York 10010, U.S.A.
Penguin Books Ltd, Harmondsworth,
Middlesex, England
Penguin Books Australia Ltd, Ringwood,
Victoria, Australia
Penguin Books Canada Limited, 2801 John Street,
Markham, Ontario, Canada L3R 1B4
Penguin Books (N.Z.) Ltd, 182–190 Wairau Road,
Auckland 10, New Zealand

First published in Penguin Books 1987
Published simultaneously in Canada

The following chapters originally appeared, in somewhat different form,
in *Between C & D* magazine: "The red high heels," "Scenes of
New York life #7," "Nunchaku" (under a different title), and "Red moon."

Grateful acknowledgment is made for permission to reprint the
following copyrighted material:
Excerpt from "Love Me Tender" by Elvis Presley and Vera Matson.
Copyright © 1956 by Elvis Presley Music.
Copyright renewed. All rights controlled by Unichappell Music, Inc.
   (Rightsong Music, Publisher).
International copyright secured.
All rights reserved. Used by permission.
Excerpt from "Non, je ne regrette rien" ("No Regrets"), lyrics by
   Michel Vaucaire, music by Charles Dumont.
Copyright © 1960, 1961, 1963 The Barclay Music Division;
   Shapiro, Bernstein & Co. Inc. Used by permission.

LIBRARY OF CONGRESS CATALOGING IN PUBLICATION DATA
Texier, Catherine.
Love me tender.
(Contemporary American fiction)
I. Title. II. Series.
PS3570.E96L6 1987   813'.54   86-25382
ISBN 0 14 01.0016 4

Printed in the United States of America by
R. R. Donnelley & Sons Company, Harrisonburg, Virginia
Set in Sabon
Designed by Gina Davis

PENGUIN BOOKS

LOVE ME TENDER

Catherine Texier was born and raised in France. She now
lives in New York City, where she is co-editor, with Joel
Rose, of *Between C&D*, a literary magazine. Her first novel,
Chloé l'Atlantique, was written in French and published in
Paris in 1983. She also co-wrote a non-fiction book, *Profes-
sion: Prostituée,* an exposé of prostitution in Quebec. One
of her short stories won Canada's McClelland & Stewart
Prize for fiction in 1979.

   Love Me Tender is her first English-language novel.

TO JOEL

*Perhaps all the wisdom, and all truth, and
all sincerity, are just compressed into that
inappreciable moment of time in which we
step over the threshold of the invisible.*

JOSEPH CONRAD,
Heart of Darkness

*Love me tender
Love me sweet
Never let me go.*

ELVIS PRESLEY, 1956

Contents

LOVE ME TENDER

The red high heels

Hot summer night. Nipples erect, hard, hard, under palms then fingertips working, intense. Moist down there where . . . The ass is taut, small and round, pushed out, thighs opened, buttocks spread out. Her breasts swell. He is a tongue. He is saliva, movement, spiraling inside her mouth tasting of sex. The tips of their tongues meet, two magnets. Two insects throwing their antennae forward in a deadly seduction dance. The tips of their tongues. They move together like fingers pressed against a mirror.

They've met at a costume party in Williamsburg, Brooklyn, where somebody dressed as a spider kept extending six black arms and legs—their long shadows played against the white brick wall like *ombres chinoises*. He had carrot hair, cropped short, and a mouth like a ripe plum. He was not in costume. He was grave, with an ironical flutter in his eyes. She, on the other hand,

1

was in costume. An eighteenth-century French marquise with her breasts propped up, having a hard time competing with the boys sporting fake breasts in outrageous *décolletés*.

Put on your red high heels, your silk bra, your garters and your smoke stockings, Julian whispers. Get dressed for me.

Jet-black in the room. Three o'clock in the morning in a Lower East Side tenement with Puerto Rican voices yelling mothafucka followed by a cascade of broken glass, and vanishing women's laughter mixed with the lingering smell of a long-dead barbecue fire.

Go ahead. Slut!

Lulu turns around slowly. Poses on one hip. Now he can vaguely make out her short blond hair pushed back to one side. Her face, white as a moon. A pink neon heart hanging from the fire escape throbs through the shades, on one of her legs.

What?

Even for fun, even for sex, she won't let him call her that.

He laughs softly.

Slut. Go get dressed for me.

Walking across the Williamsburg Bridge on a moonless night, blinded by the lights lacing downtown Manhattan. His hips moved like a dancer's, like a street boy's. His hand fumbled on the layers of taffeta and satin to grab her ass.

I'd like to fuck you right here.

She got wet in the crotch.

The wide skirts made it easy. She was not wearing underpants. When they were finished he pissed over the railing down toward the dark river on which the lights were running an oily dance.

We have to do it again, he said. And in a whisper: I will make you come next time.

That did it for her. First time a man even noticed. She was not going to let this one slip away easily.

I saw you with him! yells the man in the street.

Saw what! You were drunk. A drunken son-of-a-bitch! I told you. *Hijo de puta.*

Liar! You fucking liar.
Maricón!

He turns on the fan. His cock limp from the interruption. She shuffles through her clothes in the dark. Close to the window, he lifts up the shade. Even on tiptoes he can't see the sidewalk on their side of the street because of the fire escape. He hears someone running.

She walks back from the bathroom. Strong, confident steps of sexy high heels clapping on the bare wood floor.

I can't even see you. She laughs a throaty laugh. No, don't turn on the light.

In the dark she is on him, her hands on his shoulders, down his smooth chest, the cold, cool leather of her shoes against his thighs. He pulls a breast slowly out of the bra, feels the bulge, reaches for the nipple with his lips.

She moans. He moves his mouth down, down the loose silk of her pants, loose enough to provide a space in which he inserts a tongue, probes with a finger. In Luang Prabang, Laos, he had fucked a prostitute with red high heels which made her swing, a tight miniskirt, and a length of black lace stockings in between. She had laughed and giggled when he had gone down on her.

Mothafucka! Goddam mothafucka!

Then there was this picture from the Vietnam war he had recently seen in a pulp magazine. Vietnamese girls making it with American soldiers. All crew cut, clean-cut—as much as you could make out from the picture, because one couldn't really see their faces—their cocks erect, three or four of them in one room, the girls naked, straddling them, breasts high and full. The girls laughing together, patiently waiting to be finished off, making themselves comfortable on the mouths sucking them.

She moans. Legs spread out. Moving her ass up and down.

I love it.

You're a fucking junkie! screams the woman. Where is the money? Did you give him the money?

. . .

Sweet buttocks clad in silk. Ass all over his mouth. He bites. He
licks. The fabric is an instant stimulant/irritant. Her breasts hang
heavy in his hands. His hands maddeningly light, soft, refusing
to squeeze, to tear apart.

Oh boy!

Wiggling her breasts, wiggling her ass. His cock, hard, looking
for flesh, anything, to bury itself. He slaps her. His nails bite
into her back.

Ouch!

Outside a flurry of words in Spanish erupts, rousing screams
from the street.

Have you ever been whipped?

Jesus Christ!

Have you?

Ouch! Stop it! You're hurting me!

I want to tie you up and give it to you real good.

Are you crazy? Let me go!

Fucking bastard!

And then . . . Was it a gun? Usually it's a busted muffler. Or
a firecracker.

He has freckles on his hands. Just a few. Very light. She noticed
them the second time. His skin is pale and creamy, even on his
chest. His touch causes her flesh to tremble, lines of sweat to
ooze where his fingers have been.

He appears in the middle of the night, slim figure on the
doorstep, and vanishes at dawn. Sometimes for days. Weeks
once.

His hands—you can't see the freckles in the dark, he doesn't
like to have the light on when they make love at her place, other
than the neon heart throbbing across the floor—his hands slam
down hard on her backside.

You little . . .

He's got her tight between his knees. His nails run quick lines
of pain down her shoulder blades.

Stop it! This isn't funny!

Don't you love it?

The sneer he has sometimes. His lips curling up on very white, narrow teeth.

It's a gun. A gun has gone off. A scream. Intense. Isolated. People running, somebody tripping on a garbage can. The shrill of a woman's voice.

Let go of me. Didn't you hear?

What?

The nails stop digging. But he keeps a tight grip on her arms.

Wasn't it a gun?

A gun? You're crazy!

Didn't you hear?

Yeah. Must've been a firecracker.

No. Let me go.

Dead silence in the street. They get up, stand by the window, lift up the shade a tiny bit.

A small crowd has gathered. A body lying across the sidewalk has been half-covered with a shirt. Blood trickles down into the gutter. An ambulance howls down the block. Eight police cars block the corner, their lights throwing angry flashes of red on nearby buildings.

Is it . . . the man?

What man?

You know . . . the couple fighting . . .

Who knows, he says, a hand cupping a breast, free over the thin bra strap, pulling her toward the rumpled sheets.

Fucking junkies!

Scenes of New York life # 7

It's another sweltering, smoggy evening. Street lights dance through the mist, the gutters smell of silt and overripe garbage, the stench of a South American town around the marketplace. The leaves on the trees glisten. Getting off the air-conditioned bus Lulu feels as if she is sinking into a marsh.

Walking quickly down Avenue A, an overstuffed black nylon backpack strapped on her naked shoulders, she turns on a side street and steps into an old decayed building. Pedro! a voice yells from an open window. A woman's voice that strains her vocal capacities, broken up by endless screams. Pedro! *Dond'está?*

She lets herself into a top-floor apartment, works the three locks easily even though she's never been here before. Smell of cat piss. Red neon blinking CUCHIF ITOS reflected from across the street on the kitchen wall. Bustle of cockroaches scrambling for cracks. When she turns on the light her eyes are staring at a three-leg wooden chair painted sky blue with black-and-white zebra stripes. She drops her pack on it, walks through the three rooms strung end to end. The furniture is spare, on a worn linoleum covered floor: two pale-green plastic armchairs, 1955 style, a black vinyl sofa, foam bursting through the seams. She eases into it, kicking off her ballet slippers, when the phone starts to ring.

Lulu is scared of Julian. He keeps a switchblade underneath his mattress. He goes to Tompkins Square Park at night, his blood pounding, looking for nothing in particular, but clutching his blade, deep in a pocket of his big overcoat, *sur le qui-vive*. Adrenaline pumping, high with fear he hides in a dark corner. All of a sudden I saw this junkie walking toward me, he says. I wanted to feel the open blade in my hand. I wanted to know what it was like to pull out a weapon at a perfect stranger in the night.

Did you?

He came up to me, blocked my way and asked for my money. It was a white guy, his teeth chattering, sick with terror and strung out. I pulled out the blade, but he didn't wait to see it glitter in my hand. He ran. Man, did he run!

Hi! Is Mario there?

No. No Mario here. Sarah's the name of the person who sublet her the apartment. Maybe Mario is a friend of hers. The voice insists. But he told me he would be here now . . .

What number are you calling?

The number is right. She reads it on the dial.

Wrong number, she says.

The phone rings again. It's a man's voice this time.

Could I speak to Mario please?

No Mario here. Wrong number I told you!

Excuse me, miss, but aren't you at . . .

The address is right too. She feels hot all of a sudden. But it could be a friend of Sarah's. She says:

No, I am at . . .

She invents an address.

But I know it's Mario's number, I am sure of it, she can hear the woman from the previous phone call, in the background.

Never mind, says the man. He hangs up.

My mother died on a bitter cold January night after having given birth to me. She was alone with my aunt in the hospital, my father had disappeared months before, and she fainted when she started to push. They had to pull me out with the forceps. When she came to, a pain in her chest doubled her over, and she died from what they thought was cardiac arrest on the way to the Emergency Room. My aunt took me home with her.

You know, we are looking for somebody very professional, says the director of the dance company. Not only with perfect technique, but discipline and punctuality as well. In other words, somebody we can rely on.

Maybe she should have put a dress on or pants. Not these shorts, showing her legs, so high up.

I thought you were very good the other day. You still have a lot to learn, of course, but you have grace, energy. And for a dancer, that's what matters . . .

She wonders if it matters. If anything matters. Her mind races, to freeze her fear. *Un petit tour, deux petits tours, trois petits tours.* She is on a merry-go-round, straddling a white horse with a flaming mane. It's a beautiful old merry-go-round, its gilding peeling off, with deep reds, faded pinks, blues turning grey. She is looking at her father, whose face is half turned toward the crowd, she can only see the line of his chin, his cheekbone. He seems to be watching somebody out there. He looks younger, dreamy, very far away. She gets scared. She grasps the shiny, very smooth metal post running through the horse's head with one hand, waves at him with the other. Daddy! He doesn't hear her, the music is too loud. The merry-go-round picks up speed. She feels the wind lifting her hair around her temples. She hangs on to the post with both her hands. Daddy! Next turn, he waves at her, smiling.

Yes, I know what you mean. All I can tell you is what I told you already, I trained in Paris, I studied ballet, then when I came to the States I started doing modern dance. I danced professionally with a company in Montreal and in San Francisco, I brought you my résumé, like you asked . . .

He looks tired, his grey hair is falling in his eyes. He discreetly moves his thighs about, pulls at his jeans, stretches his arms on the back of his chair, obviously to air his armpits, the hairs of which she can see, long and damp, through the armholes of his T-shirt. He takes the envelope she brought with her, opens it, glances at the papers, the reference letters, hands them back to her.

Good, very good . . .

He is not looking at her, but at the crowd thick on the avenue. He hits the table with the flat of his hand.

Well, we'll see.

He calls the waitress, fumbles in his back pockets for his wallet, leaves some change on the table for the tip.

Listen, I have to think about it. I'll call you, okay?

Sure. Don't call me, I'll call you. Tough luck . . .

She sees these long red marks running from Julian's shoulder blades down to his waist. He tells her he fell on his back, scratched it to the quick. She knows he is lying. She saw the whip in a closet, along with a pair of handcuffs. He wakes up after dusk, heads for the dark streets, small clubs, after-hour bars by the river, brushes against the warehouse walls oozing with meat blood, under the hooks, collapses in bed in full daylight, his skin gets paler and paler. Across the street from his apartment is an abandoned synagogue, gutted to the bones, a two-dimensional movie-set façade against the deep blue sky. Pigeons fly in and out, shitting on the old portico. She gets to stare at them all day.

The phone rings furiously. In her dream it was the siren of a boat hooting through the fog in mid-Atlantic. Her clock reads 3:45 A.M. It keeps ringing and she lies flat on her back. It is sitting on the floor, on the other side of the room. Finally she crawls to pick it up, looking behind her shoulder as if surrounded by dark forces.

Listen bitch, says the voice. We know this is Mario's phone number. We know where you are. We know you are hiding him or covering him up. Don't fuck with us, bitch . . . You don't know what you are exposing your juicy little pussy to!

She stays with the receiver in her hand awhile after they hang up on the other side of the line.

Henry is tall, with a strong beaked nose, a stubble of grey beard around his ruddy face. He has a thin mouth, long and sinuous, its sensuality comes through its mobility, its greed, as he is about to kiss her, tongue glistening, his body pounding against hers.

His cock is the longest she has ever seen. It impales her, opens her up all the way to her cervix. Once he tore her skin up as he entered her. It bled and she had to go to the doctor's because it got infected. *His* doctor, uptown, on Park Avenue, who took advantage of the situation to leave his gloved finger in her cunt a little longer than a simple examination required. Everything about Henry is larger than life. His sexual appetites fascinate her. He has a live-in maid who gives him blow jobs when she brings him breakfast in bed. A girl with a turned-up nose and short black hair, a gold cross hanging between her full breasts. He told Lulu he liked women with big breasts and wide shoulders. The rumors go he seduces his friends' wives in the backseats of their cars or in the ladies' room during parties. He is obsessed with sex. He paints stretched-out crotches with sweaty pubic hair in brash purples and bleeding reds next to Marilyn Monroe or Doris Day look-alike faces floating in midair. He is obsessed with the poses of sex. A woman's body lying upside down on a flight of stairs, neck outstretched, red lips open to glittering white teeth. Not a bad artist. Quite fashionable as a matter of fact. A flashy reputation climaxing with a house in the Hamptons and a two-story loft in Tribeca. He fucks her in the elevator going up to his loft, he fucks her on his king-size bed with a view of New Jersey sunsets, on the beach in the Hamptons at 2 A.M. Makes her come in Times Square movie theaters, his Burberry raincoat spread over their knees, makes her walk up the stairs leading to his mezzanine with no pants on and black net stockings held up by garters and pushes a finger up her crotch. She complies.

In the cab on their way back from Eighty-sixth Street where they went to buy German *wurst* and pastries (his parents are from Berlin) Henry's got his hand in her pants. He can't resist asserting his power over women in public spaces. Once at a luncheon at the Waldorf where he had managed to have her invited with him—Remember the rule, no underwear!—he had made her come with his fingers *entre la poire et le fromage*. They go to her place. Sometimes he gets a kick out of straying in the back alleys of the city, as he puts it.

The phone is ringing when she unlocks the door.

Listen. Mario's looking for you. He says he can't stand it watching you come up with foreign men to his apartment.

What is it, asks Henry.

Nothing, she says, bending to loosen his belt.

She burns next to Julian, wet, her joints aching, nipples erect. He lies awake in the dark, motionless, stiff, his blade by his side. Once he tells her to loop a silk ribbon around his neck and pull when he starts coming. She won't do it. Do it, he says. No. He flies into a rage. He doesn't touch her anymore. Sometimes he won't come back for days on end. She finds him lying naked spread-eagled across the mattress, dead asleep, one hand hooked over his cock as if for protection.

Henry makes her listen to a tape of fucking sounds he has recorded with another lover, a blond in a tight navy-blue silk dress and high-heeled pumps who was leaving the loft as Lulu arrived. It's like a doctor's office, Lulu says instead of coming as he expected her to, breaking up in giggles when she realizes he has taped the session that same afternoon. He laughs with her but isn't sure he likes her tone. With one finger he hits the Off button on the tape recorder and whispers *Ich liebe dich* . . .

Red fear

FEAR   MIEDO

RED   ROJA

FEAR   MIEDO

reads the sign on Houston Street. Mystique catches it from the rear bus window. In red block letters dripping with paint, a circle crossed like a French one-way sign in the middle on the white-washed wall and the RED FEAR hot red, so red it seems to be blinking. Her breath quickens. Red Fear. Black plague. Gay plague. Yellow fever. Bloody Monday. Ash Wednesday. Black Sunday. Seven Days' War. And the Marines killed in Lebanon for nothing.

Red Fear means coming back from playing volleyball and finding her father clutching his chest in front of his gas station and seeing him collapse by one of the pumps. Red Fear means watching his body on the stretcher disappear feet last in the ambulance and asking, is Daddy going to die, Mom? Red Fear her own breathless life—literally, no air, living at the top of her lungs, the gigs every other night, her three rooms lined up like three overstuffed jewelry boxes, twenty years of junk, mainly in the form of discarded clothes billowing in double-strength garbage bags shooting out from the walls, from the floors, pushed in the closets, under the bed, forever growing back, you always tripped on something or other. No man in her bed for three months. Once she went on for a year without a man. A whole year. She thought that it was the end of her life. That you could die without sex. She didn't die. But she lived wretchedly. She was utterly depressed. Then she had a short affair with a woman, which made her ache even more for a man, and she thought she lacked imagination.

Red Fear wrings the guts of young women at night alone in strange apartments they sublet for a few weeks when they arrive in town, barely getting by. Red Fear when you hear the wind crackling through the branches, the windows rattling, and you think a faceless man is climbing up the fire escape, his feet bouncing silently on his sneakers' rubber soles. You wake up staring in the dark, peering hard, trying to make out this distinct sound through the wind, the trucks swooshing by in the light rain. You can almost see the hand holding the blade, smell the sweat through the dirty jeans moving along the bed. The mattress is on the floor. He is towering over you. He is dressed in dark colors, he blurs into the night. He breathes hard. You are nailed to the bed. A silent scream infinitely echoes in waves through your body. You don't want to die like that. It can't be true. You listen with all your pores. You are a radar aroused by fear. You don't flee, don't yell, you turn into an electric arc of slashing perceptions, wishing to have a yogi's power to vanish into thin air. You think your only way of fighting is to strive to become invisible. His breathing dies with the wind. The rain has stopped too. You turn on the light. There's the familiar sight of your clothes spilling out of a suitcase half-open on the floor, and piled in a soft heap on a chair. The cat yawns and stretches a lazy

13

paw, attempting to push a cockroach scurrying for cover along a crack in the floor.

Lulu lifts up her head from Julian's crotch, a hair on her tongue that she peels off between two fingers. He's got strawberry-blond pubic hair that smells like honey, a long cock turned upwards. What are you doing? he says. Go on. Nobody's ever done it to me like that. Never? Never quite like that. He pushes her down on his white skinny thighs. He says, *J'ai envie de capoter avec toi,* a phrase he told her he learned in Montreal. She floats over him, her wide skirt hovering about his face like a big black raven. Then his weirdly bent cock makes her come screaming loud. His dark eyes stare at her so intensely she thinks she touches something deep in him but maybe it's only her, a chink in her own armor, it must've been only her. A week later there are four of them in his apartment, stoned and drunk out of their minds. They end up on his terrace (he's got a tiny penthouse perched up on a roof like a bird's nest), their bodies in a warm heap, clothes lifted on naked skin, hands grabbing soft breasts, recesses of delicate skin, fingers pulling zippers, pulling underwear elastic, rolling T-shirts up, tongues searching for cracks, running down furrows, palms pressed softly, arousing almost silent moans. After a while it's clear Julian and the other girl are going off together. They retreat to his bedroom. Lulu and the dark-haired boy, his name's Rob, sit up breathless. He says, come on. He says, that's all right. But it's not all right. He says, let's fuck. But it's not all right. I can't, she says. They get dressed and walk to the East River Park. It's almost dawn and it smells of sea and mud. They lean against the parapet, watching a tanker slowly slide through the oily water. Lulu shudders. She says, isn't it where that woman jogger got shot the other day? Yeah. Rob puts his hand on hers. He says, well, you know, these things happen. It doesn't mean anything. But all she sees is Julian's hair tousled on the girl's shoulder and his hand lifting her skirt moving into her white panties and her thighs opening up with a twist of her hips.

. . .

14

At this point in her life, Mystique's red fear fades to a dull ache, a dull sense of impending disaster. I'm halfway there, she laughs, jokingly referring to her age, late thirties, with ironic bitterness, already putting this distance within herself, not wanting to be too closely related to this older self who, day after day, in very small ways, betrays her. You know why we are lovers? she once said to a twenty-two-year-old musician with whom she had a hot and brief affair one winter. It's because, deep down, we are the same age. Only my body looks older. He had laughed. If you hadn't told me that, he said, I wouldn't have noticed. Maybe not my body, but my face, yes! He had taken Mystique's face with both his hands, these hands Mystique thought were tortured and talented, studying her red-speckled green eyes, the deep expression lines around her mouth, the dyed-black hair rising to a brief crew cut above her forehead, then he let go and said, this is as it should be. What's better about a young face? It's only a blank page. There is no merit. Yes, but what fine skin, Mystique had replied, what flawless . . . Will you stop torturing yourself, he said.

She's not bitter though, at least not more than can be expected. Imagine someone going through life with sweet feelings as only baggage? The thought of such a candy-sweet, honey-dripping, saccharine gook makes her nauseous. She never wanted a child and she doesn't have one, she never wanted a steady man and she doesn't have one, but now she doesn't remember why she fought so hard against a straight life. Everything seems to have blurred, the acceptable and the disgusting not so clearly defined any more, except maybe her early nightmare: ending up married to a doctor, with three kids in a suburban split-level. She's come to see her life as fate rather than a struggle and yet she keeps struggling. And she still dreams of bursting out on the scene one day and she still wheels and deals and contacts and talks her way into potential deals, smokey projects, half-promises, without them she would be a middle-aged cabaret dancer stuck in-between, betraying her own axiom, you've got to go all the way, not stop in the middle, it's the most dangerous place: that's where you really get crushed.

WOMEN'S AND CHILDREN'S BODIES FOUND
IN MASS-MURDER GRAVESITE
IN CALIFORNIA

Women's and children's bodies were found near a backwoods cabin along with a horror video tape showing two men forcing a woman to comply to brutal sexual acts and threatening to kill her if she didn't. The woman begged the men to give her back her baby. Another tape showed one of the men saying that he "forced women to submit" because he wasn't attractive to them. Officials who searched the site said the cabin was stocked with guns and a cinder-block building nearby was equipped with a torture chamber.

Carefully, Lulu cuts the news item with her nail scissors, adding it to a pile of clippings she has already collected, and moves on to the next page. A full-page report states that several police officers were involved in the torture case of two Latino men arrested in a Queens precinct. Their bodies showed evidence of burns on their backs, their arms, their genitals, that could only have been inflicted by the new stun guns approved for police use, jammed against the skin like burning cigarettes, except they send unbearable electric shocks.

The photos show small black unfocused spots circled in black pencil on the backs and arms of the men. They are newspaper shots of torsos and limbs devoid of life like rare butterflies pinned on the wall for clinical observation. Lulu's just gotten up. It's two o'clock in the afternoon and she tries to boost her energy with caffeine, which sends shivers up and down her spine but doesn't propel her out of her chair. And now this, on page three of yesterday's *Daily News*. There is a pile of detective novels on the table, Raymond Chandler, Jim Thompson, James M. Cain, Dashiell Hammett, and a couple of books from Patricia Highsmith's Ripley series. She leafs through a few of them, but her eyes keep shifting back to the grey torsos in the photographs. She always reads the *News* and sometimes the *Post* or even the *National Enquirer* for the outrageous headlines that she clips. She has trouble with *The New York Times*. The tiny, sober characters float in front of her eyes in dangerous speedy moves.

They undulate. The small slanted titles telescope. The *News* is like a black-and-white neon billboard on Times Square. DEAD DEAD DEAD DEAD flashes in upper-case lower-case DEAD dead DEAD dead. Who's dead she wonders. She reads 2,500 in India, 45,000 in Pakistan, hundreds of thousands in Ethiopia. She reads STOP COMMUNISM STOP COMMUNISM STOP COMMUNISM. She reads HOUSE OK'S $38M TO AID NICA REBELS. Then REAGAN. REAGAN DEAD REAGAN DEAD. Wishful thinking, she sighs. She can't read past the headlines. The lines dissolve into a blurry mass of black ink. But the huge type and the photos are like a photoplay of death. She clips the article about the police torture and tosses the newspaper on the floor. She picks up the *Village Voice*, in which she likes to read the Personals. This one, for instance:

> Married 43 yr old JM. Mellow, handsome, witty. My mistress of 22 years died. I seek to renew that enduring romance when I finish my mourning. Slim, attractive (24–45) female respond.

Or that one:

> Carribean Queen sought by BM, 45, lawyer. Desires relation-ship with female 20–45, 200 lbs +.

And this:

> 77TH STREET RR LINE BAY RIDGE
> I see you every day between 6 and 8 P.M., when you buy your tokens. I think you're gorgeous, but the rules prevent me from telling you so. If you'd be at all interested, write me or slip me a note with your money some evening! Johnny.

One of these days she'll answer an ad like this and see what happens.

A Japanese woman from San Francisco, whose husband had taken a mistress, took her two children to the Pacific Ocean and walked into the sea with them to commit suicide, says a radio report drifting in through Lulu's open window from her neighbor's apartment. She stops reading to listen. In Japanese culture, it is so shameful for a woman to be betrayed by her husband that she must commit suicide and, according to the local code of honor, take her children with her. People who were on the beach saw them and alerted the Coast Guard. But the children were already dead. The woman was still alive. She now faces prosecution for first-degree murder of her children. The prosecutor, a woman, said this is the United States, not Japan, and the court system doesn't recognize other cultures' codes. The Japanese woman is pleading not guilty, the radio announcer concludes, but there is no such thing as not guilty for reasons of cultural difference.

From the Personals Lulu moves to the rest of the Classifieds. She falls on this ad:

> Writer seeks young Frenchwomen recently arrived in the States for interviews and research. Perfectly legit. Small pay.

There is a phone number in Manhattan, an Upper West Side number. It would be easy money, she would meet a fancy uptown writer. She clips the ad, fingers it for a moment and pins it on her bulletin board behind the kitchen table. Then she proceeds to circle all the ads for waitresses and barmaids and gets ready to leave her house.

Hi, beautiful, Ed says, poking a bedroom face at the dressing-room door. What brings you in so early?

Mystique shrugs, ignoring the question. What's the matter, Eddie, you didn't get any sleep last night?

Why?

Or do you think you look cute with those eyes?

He laughs, innuendos aplenty behind this smile of his, eyebrows arched in a telling way.

Been up all night having fun again, huh?

Eyebrows arch one more time. Wanna do a line before the customers come in?

No thanks. Never before work. You know me. Not a drug addict like some of us.

Ciao, baby.

'Bye.

The Blue Night's overcrowded dressing room reeks of cold cigarette smoke and stale beer. It's a small room leading to a dirty toilet at the back of the stage, with frilly dresses hung on a rack for the drag-queen number alternating with the go-go girls' act. Boas, sequined tops, red and black nylon G-strings, wigs and high-heel pumps size fourteen and above are scattered on the floor, along with stuffed bras and a couple of peach satin girdles 1945 model. The walls are pasted with *Life* covers from the fifties, magazine clippings of movie stars and dated ads. The mirror, evenly lit with small pinkish bulbs, sucking up shadows and lines, sends off an approving reflection of Mystique's face, and she likes to sit on a ripped plastic chair, wrapped up in an old Japanese silk robe, doing her toenails or smoking a cigarette. There life comes to a halt and complete silence. The dressing room is a glittering tomb encased in the dark pit of the club still closed before the evening, the front bar dimly lit, deserted except for Ed, the Blue Night's stage manager and head barman, cleaning up the counter and straightening the bottles in front of the back-wall mirror.

Mystique opens her makeup jars and starts spreading the white foundation on her cheeks up to her lashes and works it deep down her neck, making her face like that of a Kabuki performer until the carefully painted red and blue triangles explode from her cheekbones to her temples.

Ed is at the door again. You look like Grace Jones, he sneers, stirring her from the deep well in which she's sunk, dulling her pleasure, clipping her energy. Hey, there's a girl at the bar who's interested in Marita's part.

How did she know about Marita?

She didn't. She stopped by for the barmaid's job. She had no experience as a barmaid but it turns out she's a dancer. You want to see her?

Did she talk to Marty yet?

Yeah. He says it's your ballgame.

What's she like?

She looks the part. Which doesn't mean a thing, of course.

Looking the part is half of it. Okay, bring her in.

Lulu sees the death mask face, the purple lips outlined in black, the red and blue marks slashed across the face emerging from the old faded kimono, the bare feet with bright fuschia nail polish, the hand signaling to a chair piled with accessories.

Don't mind the mess, Mystique says. Just make some room on the chair.

Lulu looks like a teenager freshly escaped from home, yet there's a toughness in her and knowing eyes, scared but determined, competent hands, small and tight body, style stripped down to its essence, sneaks, jeans, T-shirt, balanced in a kind of perfection, tight here, loose there, colors faded, unself-conscious yet controlled, and Mystique doesn't try to probe, question, test, she lets Lulu's presence refocus the room, bring out its dust, its tackiness, its sloppiness and stir her own despair, her near-panic at time closing door after door every day. She doesn't talk much and observes Lulu a lot. Ed is wrong, Mystique finally decides, she isn't the part, but she can play it.

The Blue Night Lounge

The Blue Night Lounge occupies the ground floor and basement of an old tenement at the edge of Tribeca and the Wall Street area. The whole façade of the building is painted blue, sky blue with deep purple window frames and a night-blue door, above which a purple neon sign underlined with baby blue flashes THE BLUE NIGHT in curved letters. Inside, a small, cozy barroom, with a long oak bar harnessed with nickel strips running along its full length, opens on a small square back room crowded with a couple of dozen tables and a low stage. A thick velvet curtain hangs behind the door, separating the entranceway from the bar and hiding the inside of the club from the curious glances of passersby.

Patrons stand three thick along the bar waiting for the show to start as Lulu walks in, carrying a tote bag full of sequined costumes for her numbers. The back room is empty, its small round polished tables gleaming in the dim glow of a few spot-lights only partially turned on. Ed shows her into the dressing room where Mystique pulls on a pair of flesh-colored tights topped by shimmering panties. Even in summer, I never dance completely naked, she explains to Lulu. Tights make the skin look smoother, tighter. They give a nicer line to the legs. She rummages through Lulu's bag, choosing appropriate outfits for the show. I went to Forty-second Street for that one, Lulu says, as Mystique approves a silver-spangled G-string held by a rhine-stone bow on the hip. A man, whom Mystique introduces as Poupée, is worming his wide shoulders and thick waist into a sheath of shocking pink satin and adjusts a jet-black wig that cascades past his shoulder blades. From the dressing-room cur-tain, they watch Poupée's six-foot frame sway to center-stage on his high-heeled snake pumps while his gloved hand clutches a tiny black velvet purse to his bosom. He intones Edith Piaf's *Non, je ne regrette rien*, and the room starts rustling.

Non, rien de rien
Non, je ne regrette rien
Ni le bien qu'on m'a fait, ni le mal
Tout ça m'est bien égal
Non, rien de rien . . .

They love it. When Poupée ends the number, nursing the mike to his lips, the crowd goes bananas. At the peak of the bravos Lulu and Mystique crisscross the stage dressed as French cancan girls in pink and black swishing silk. They come back in fake pink panther fur coats and dance face-to-face as if one was a reflection of the other in a mirror. They wear the same style wig, platinum silver with a blunt cut and thick straight bangs down to their eyelids. They look at each other the way you check the circles under your eyes and the state of your makeup after a long night of partying. Then they throw their coats behind them on the floor and slowly undress, buckles unbuckling and zippers going down and buttons unbuttoning and snaps popping and hooks unclasping and slips slipping and suspender belts loosening and stockings rolling down, teasing the patrons with suggestive swaying of the hips and tilting of the chins. When they strip down their mandarin-orange panties to reveal teeny sequined G-strings and remove their bras to show small silver cups sprouting a tuft of white ostrich feathers, then bend toward each other till their lips touch as if kissing a mirror, ecstasy turns to delirium. Men drunk with beer crawl to the edge of the stage and wave folded dollar bills trying to stuff them in their crotches. Is this for real? Lulu asks, as they run offstage, leaving heaps of discarded clothes behind them. Mystique says there're always a couple of drunks on Saturday nights and unscrews a bottle of seltzer at the makeup table. But this is a cabaret, not a topless bar, they have to show restraint. If they give any hint of trying to climb onstage, Marty, the manager, unleashes the bouncers.

You were great, say Sirouelle and Andrée as they are getting ready for the punk number, which they do with Mystique after intermission. Lulu, you were a real pro, you looked as if you'd been doing it for years.

Yes, Lulu sighs. It already feels like years.

I have this idea about America. Oh yes? What is it? A land of fun. Of cheap fun. Awesome. A crystal ball in which you can read the future of humanity. Rock 'n' roll, sex and mental retardation. A land of hot summer nights, of scorching hot afternoons. Crowds seething along the avenues. Men's long legs bouncing on sneakers. Tight asses in sexy blue jeans. Asses. Asses. If I was only allowed one image of America it would be a closeup of a Levi Strauss—clad man's ass moving at eye level. American men in the heat of summer. Sweating. Round shoulders. Thick lips. White teeth. Dazzling smiles. Just that. Men. Childish. Watching baseball on tv and slapping their knees after a home run, yelling and sipping cans of Bud around the coffee table. The back of the hand rising to wipe off the mouth. Impeccably white T-shirt on tanned skin. Closeup of bared thighs running around the track.

. . .

Don't expect anything from anybody in this town, declares Mystique after the show, as part of her crash initiation course to Lulu. She's removing her makeup in front of the mirror scalloped with tiny pink bulbs and throwing smeared balls of cotton into the wastebasket. Did you hear me?

I've heard that so many times, sighs Lulu, who, after fingering some greasy cream pots, lights up a cigarette from a brand new pack Mystique has pulled out of her pocketbook. Sounds like a cliché to me. Yuk, she says with a distinct French accent after a few puffs, and puts it out. I hate smoking!

So don't spoil my cigarettes, honey. What's the matter, not in the mood for good and sound advice tonight?

Mystique, you sound like my aunt.

I tell you, kid! I've never had so many disappointments than in this city. And especially from people who seemed the most sensitive, supportive, friendly. I know I sound like sour grapes . . . But I tell you. Everybody is here to make it. And nobody is giving anybody else a break . . .

I find people rather helpful and supportive, on the contrary.

. . . especially those people who live on the so-called edge, Mystique continues, paying no heed to Lulu's comment. She wipes off the Vaseline with handfuls of tissue paper, moving in circular motions, from her nose to her ears and from the corner of her eyes to her temples. Especially in the so-called artistic ghetto. Too much at stake. Too much competition. Too much insecurity. And it hurts more, because you think these people are your brothers, your sisters. Sisters! Gimme a break. That's what really hurts. I did some shows in the artsy clubs. It's even worse than here. You think, that person at least, that one I know I can trust. You do any favor you can to anybody, not because you're opportunistic, mind you, I mean, not more than the next fellow, and you never get anything in return. You find yourself lucky if they don't stab you in the back. And they don't even try to spare your feelings when they do it. Anyway. Maybe it's just as well. No hypocrisy to soften the blow.

You guys are so cynical out here.

Cynical? Pass me that bottle, please, the blue plastic one, near your elbow, yeah. Thanks. I don't know. We rant and rave about this city, about America. Maybe we're just paranoid. Everybody is so fucking insecure here. It's like we all think somebody is going to step on our toes the minute we give an inch. We're so eager to get there, you know what I mean? Where? Who the fuck knows? Who the fuck cares? Where we were told we were supposed to get to. Success. Money. Beauty. Men. Women. Whatever your bag is. We're running like fucking chickens without heads. We think happiness is over the rainbow.

At least you have a dream. Where I come from, we don't have dreams. Just memories. We remember the war, the wars. The war of '70, the war of '14–18, the war of '40, the Algerian war. At the end of every dinner my grandfather used to say: one more meal the Prussians won't take away from us. The wars are like posts staking off people's lives. Every war crushed a little more of our inheritance. We're still bending down to pick up the pieces, looking at them, juggling them. See how much more they can yield. Looking for another order, another meaning. Never looking ahead. We're running out of juice. We're scared. Can I have another cigarette?

Honey, only if you're going to smoke it.

Mystique's finished removing her makeup. They both light cigarettes and smoke in silence until Lulu stubs hers out again with a face. Mystique grins reproachfully at her. She says, we had our wars too. My father was at Pearl Harbor and talked about the Japs all through my childhood. He was sorry he didn't get Europe and North Africa, like his buddy Irv who got to see Gay Paree and make out with the little women of Pigalle, instead of sweating and picking up corpses in the Philippines.

Lulu says, American men got to travel around the world like rich tourists to save the so-called free world. Occasionally like heroes. She says, I had an aunt who was twenty years old during the liberation of Paris. She remembers the American soldiers hanging out in clusters from the khaki tanks lined up along the Champs-Elysées. They were grabbing the girls and sitting them on their laps. The first boy my aunt ever kissed was an American with red hair and freckles on his face who bent over her and gave her a big smooch right on her mouth. She dreamed about him for the whole summer after that.

Lulu says, for the Americans it was a big adventure, a macho game played out in faraway lands. But in France everybody lived the wars.

How old are you?

Twenty-five. Why?

You didn't live through any of these wars. We had the Vietnam war. *I* was twenty when it started. We're still fucked up from it. The whole country is fucked.

Lulu says, I don't know. All they talked about was the war, one or the other. You people, you protect yourselves. You cultivate amnesia. We cultivate our memories. They dominate our lives.

Ed appears, flourishing a set of keys, and bangs them against the door frame. Sorry to interrupt, girls, but that's it for me. Let's go. Out. I should've left twenty minutes ago. I don't know about you, but I don't get overtime pay. Come on, let's GO!

Mystique takes her time tying a chiffon turban around her hair, saying, honey-sweety, all right, all right, cutie. You got it. And to Lulu: Ed's always in a hurry. The man doesn't believe he has enough time to live.

Lulu thinks she sees Julian on her way back from the Blue Night, his frail body dressed in black, setting off his pale skin. She recognizes his slender shaven neck, his quick, tight step. But when she catches up with him, a man with a bored face she's never seen before stares at her and turns the corner. She's left watching a bum, his hat made of layers of brown paper bags and old newspapers, bent at the waist over a garbage can, rummaging through rotted fruits, heaps of discarded clothes, looking for cardboards to make himself a bed on a doorstep. She avoids him, circles around his body at a distance, all the way to the edge of the sidewalk. She thinks he smells of fermented flesh.

. . .

Hi, says Henry's voice on the line as she walks in. Did you just get back from the club? Will you come down? I'll send a cab for you. I have a surprise. Don't ask. Come as you are, but remember the rule!

As she is about to leave, the phone rings again.

It's Mario, says a deep, muffled voice. I am waiting for you downstairs, in the cab. We're gonna have fun, you and me . . .

River view

The yellow cab, a Checker, is double-parked in front of Lulu's building. She walks to the driver's door, peeks in. White teeth flashing in the dark. Honest face, mid-thirties, questioning, a man doing his job, wondering what that lady wants, ask him if he'll go out of town, luggage to take down the stoop, wait for her boyfriend?

She sees the black moustache, the mass of curly black hair. She's ready to flee, run back into the building.

Who are you? she asks.

Is that what you usually ask cab drivers? I drive a cab, lady. Radio call to pick up someone at this address. He looks at the sheet clipped on a board, next to him on the seat, then up to the top of the wooden door, to the three metal figures dangling on three nails. Two-oh-five. Right. Are you the party who called for a cab?

No. I mean, yes, I guess the cab is for me.

So get in, miss.

She stands by the door, hesitant.

Is your name Mario?

Hey, lady! You want this ride, yes or no?

Please. I need to know.

The cabbie hits the gear shift, about to press the accelerator pedal. No, he says, name's José. You getting in or not?

Yes, she says, letting herself in.

The evening is warm but breezy. The smell of the sea. A lightness in the air reminiscent of Carribean shores. Henry's sitting on a high stool in front of his drawing table, turned sideways toward the wall of windows of his loft. He watches the intense sky turning indigo over the river. He watches the boats, flat heavy tankers heading for the docks, for the tip of Manhattan, maybe the Brooklyn piers. He watches the string of lights dancing along the Jersey shore. He looks like a big bird of prey perched on a high branch, his nose royal, his mouth set tight.

He has started a new project, suggested to him by a publisher friend, a kind of erotic daybook, an artist's book, printed in a limited edition, on expensive creamy parchment and sold at a high price to selected collectors. The texts, which he originally wanted to write himself, for he boasts of an as-yet unrecognized literary talent, are to be, by decision of his editor, excerpts from works by Bataille, de Sade, from *Histoire d'O* and other French erotic classics.

But he is not thinking of this assignment, even though sheets of paper are spread on the table, and sketches of tumescent cocks and hairy vulvae have been drawn in charcoal, next to female and male figures in lascivious poses.

He is not thinking of Lulu either, who must be on her way to his place, but of another woman, very young, whom he met that same afternoon in the subway, which he never takes usually, it must have been fate, an omen from the gods. They've exchanged phone numbers and he felt his cock swell the front of his pants and saw her eyes go moist and he knows for sure they'll be lovers, but not yet, let her stew a day or two, then he thought of Lulu later as he was taking a bath and of something he'd never done with her, and he sent a cab for her so that she wouldn't have an excuse for not coming.

Who is Mario, Lulu asks, sitting carefully on the couch across from Henry's drawing table. He's been showing her his latest drawings, she has feigned a polite interest.

What do you mean, Mario? Am I supposed to know a Mario?

I don't know. I'm asking you.

Not as far as I know.

You don't know a Mario who is a cabdriver?

Lulu. I used to have lots of friends who drove hacks, including me. But no more. A shame, no doubt. The only Mario I know, come to think of it, is Dragan's doorman. You know, Dragan, the sculptor?

Lulu shakes her head. Never mind. Forget it.

Henry slips next to her, a tumbler of Scotch in his hand, pushing a gin and tonic in front of her.

Thanks, she says, taking a long cold sip.

His hand creeps up her leg under the long skirt, up her stocking, under her garter. She doesn't feel the rush, blood pounding low down her belly, vulva swelling, flesh rising to the feel of the hand. Her skin shrinks under his fingers, tightens, recedes, the surface cold as marble. Heart of stone, heavy. But her crotch betrays her. There is the familiar tingling, a tightening of the vaginal walls, pure reflex caused by the hand brushing the tender white flesh on the inside of her thigh, both thighs now, way high, parting them a little, and her letting them open, feeling herself get moist and she wants to slap him in the face but she lets him work his way up there, lets him peel her clothes off, zip his fly open, his pants, push his underwear down his legs. He's big for her, it moves her, she lowers herself down on him, her lips brushing his. He looks every bit his forty-five years, skin coarsened, loosened around the eyes. She teases him with her breasts, the small ivory cornucopia he's given her dangling between them.

When they lie on the couch later watching the night, she thinks she should have plucked his hand off her and pushed it on his lap. He sits up to get his drink and his belly ripples over his thighs. Then he lies back, scratching his crotch looking satisfied.

On the way to his loft, the cab had stopped for a red light and an old woman had crossed the street. She was so old, so parched that you didn't think it was a woman really, just an ancient animal. She walked very slowly, with difficulty, and didn't make it to the other side of the street before the light turned green, the cab had to give a light honk to hurry her. Lulu had looked at her feet, purple toes with large long nails like claws spread on open sandals, alligator feet, prehistoric feet.

Lulu gets up and goes to the bathroom to take a shower.

We were all sitting around the lawn behind the garage at the farmhouse where my father's family spent all their summers. The parents playing bridge in the living room. All little kids, four, five years old. The oldest ones were riding their bikes or playing volleyball at the net set up by the back garden wall. Ivy grew on it. I remember the holly bushes on either side of the garage door. There were more boys than girls. Don't remember their names, what they looked like. Oh, yes, one was Annie. Name stuck with me. The baker's daughter. A redhead with a page-boy haircut. We thought she was ugly, big thick mouth and dirty fingernails. My grandmother's opinion. Then the boys asked us girls to pull down our pants. The others must've done it. Me too. But to me a total blank. Don't remember what I showed, and if I did. Only the guilt afterwards. Me sitting on the sidewalk all alone in front of the house, knees pulled up to chin, arms wrapped around legs.

Come on over, Henry says. Satisfied. His drink drained. Both arms folded behind his neck. Motioning to the couch with his toes. What's the matter? Why are you getting dressed? Aren't you spending the night?

Unh-unh. Gotta go home. Get up early tomorrow morning.

Why not the truth. That his age showed. And his prick not so glorious anymore wrinkled under his potbelly. He has a certain stature though. Standing up, getting himself a white terry robe, his blue eyes piercing, wrapping his arms around her shoulders. We should spend some time together, he says. Maybe a weekend in the Hamptons. You and me by ourselves. Quiet. Nobody around. No social life.

Henry, I'm going home.

Let me call a cab for you. At this time out here. You'll have to walk all the way over to Sixth Avenue. Pretty deserted.

No. No cab. I need the walk.

You're beautiful, he says, his hand slipping down from the small of her back to her buttocks.

Charles was the name of the first man who made me come. I was sixteen. He was middle-aged, or so I thought. He gave me head in his Citroën DS 19 in a little wood outside Paris where hookers hung out along the main road. He did it well and I wanted more. He said I was sensual. I liked that. Then I met his friend, and I don't remember *his* name, only his navy suit, his black hair curling in the neck, his Porsche, the silver chain around his wrist. He took me to a nightclub in a sleazy part of town. I let him put his hand up my thigh. Then we went to his "crib," as he called it. He thought he had it made with me. He left me in the living room, excused himself. Then called me from the bathroom. He was taking a shower, talked to me through the curtain, vapor coming up the ceiling. He opened the curtain a notch, making sure I got a good look at his endowments, invited me to step in with him. I said I didn't feel like it. He left the curtain pulled back, water spraying in fine drops so I had to move back one step, toweled himself. Rough, puffing. Then he slipped on a robe, leaving it open in front. Come here, he said, pushing the door to his bedroom. Maybe I wanted it, I don't know. I followed him. He said, make yourself comfortable. Let me get your drink. I sat on the side of the bed, knees close together, my chin on my closed fist. He came back and sat down next to me, started his number again with his hand. By that time I was finished with him. I stood up. He said, what do you think you're doing, or something like that. I said, I'm going. He stood up too and pushed me on the bed. I didn't yell, I just rolled over on my knees so that he wouldn't get a hold on me. He did. He yanked my legs open, pulled down my panties, I heard the fabric tear. I kicked him, kicked in the air. I got hysterical. I was sobbing like a kid, he slapped me in the face. He let me gasp, then came back with a glass of iced water. He slipped his arms around my shoulders and put the glass to my lips. There, he said, you'll feel better; take it easy. I calmed down. He said, lie down, just let yourself go, you don't have to do anything, I'll do all the work. I let him do it. I had lost my nerve. I didn't want him to hit me again. Better get it over with quick. How bad could it be? He was hot on the trail and hard—a short stubby prick that spilled its stuff as soon as he got it in me. I looked for my panties, they were ripped, and I pushed them in my raincoat pocket and let him take me to the door. Bye, he said. I didn't say anything. I waited at the elevator door. Then I noticed one of my earrings was missing.

I almost rang his bell to get it back.

Bye, Henry says at the door.

Lulu looks at him, his ruddy complexion, his jovial smile. He goes to pet her ass again. She swiftly moves away, ignores the elevator, heads for the staircase.

Salvine

Julian is standing naked in the middle of his bedroom, the lights dimmed, the city blurred silver in the foggy night outside his windows. He walks around, a small notebook in his hand, looking for a good spot. Tries sitting cross-legged on the floor, leaning at a window, lying across the bed. Finally settles for a wall. He leans against it, his ribs protruding slightly over his caved-in stomach, one foot hooked behind the other. He is positioned in such a way that he has a good view of himself reflected in the full-length mirror on the opposite wall. He reads from the notebook, which is covered by a tight handwriting, no margin, lines running from edge to edge, the pages worn out at the corners. He reads a poem and then reads it again several times, adjusting the level of his voice and the slump of his spine, balancing his hips this way or that. At his right, a tv screen, the

34

sound off, carries out a dance of quick closeups of women's faces, succeeding each other like witnesses on a stand.

Salvine is waiting for him downstairs in a car parked outside his building. He calls her his mistress, to single her out from his other lovers, a rich glamorous woman with a voluptuous body, twice his age, no strings attached. As if relationships could be officially negotiated. There is the verbal contract and there is the real one. He feels a string pull sharply when the buzzer rings and he deliberately takes his time getting dressed and snapping a gold stud at his ear before walking down. As Salvine bends to open up the door on the passenger's side, he finds himself wrapped in her arms loaded by loops of gilded chains, pressed against her soft breasts. He reaches for her throat with his lips.

Long time no see, Julian, she says, shortening the -ee with a slight accent. What were you doing? I have been waiting for at least ten minutes.

Someone called. Couldn't hang up.

I've been missing you, she says, stroking his fingers, then squeezing them gently. So, what's up?

He sighs, leans against the seat.

I've been writing poetry.

Poetry? What happened to your band?

Broke up. Just a couple weeks ago. Fucked-up business. Where are we going?

A new place by the river. They serve game.

He makes a face.

They'll probably have steak if you can't stomach wild boar. They're also supposed to have exceptional Bourgogne. Sound better?

She looks at him, runs her hand on his shaven nape, up against the hair growth.

He nods to the door as the car slows down in front of a gold canopy.

That the place?

Yep.

. . .

35

They make a stunning couple as they step into the crowded doorway. She, with the allure of a fifties star, hiding behind dark glasses. He, trailing behind her, unmistakably younger, the boyishness of his short reddish-blond hair accentuated by his black suit.

She throws her shawl of powder-blue and wine cashmere on the back of a chair, but keeps the turban casually tied around her head, letting a few strands of hair loose on her forehead. He sits in front of her, at a small table covered with starched white linen and clear crystals, tucked near a window. The restaurant is bustling with voices that the customers maintain at a relatively discreet sound level, appropriate to their wealth and social standing.

Salvine's elegance is composed, mastered, hiding a deep terror cleverly camouflaged. She has a beauty mark at the corner of her lips. Sometimes she looks like a marquise from King Louis XIV's court, or like Madame Récamier, her forehead encircled with a ribbon she chooses of emerald or crimson velvet. She has hips and too much stomach, the middle of her body hides under the black dress, eludes the eye, avoids asserting itself, but, above the calfskin heels, she has exquisite ankles delicately hosed in lavender silk.

No way, she says suddenly, cutting short their conversation. *A aucun prix*. Refusing even to consider the sale of the house she owns in the Catskills and that turns out to give her more headache than pleasure. And yet I am a city girl, she adds, laughing. I get sick in the country.

Julian takes her hand and presses it between his palms.

Beyond the windowpane the sky is neon orange, bleeding New Jersey. She clicks her heels, discreetly, as she crosses her legs.

At no price. And yet she pays the price. She pays the price with the chronic bronchitis that chokes her lungs. She spent the humid winters in Poitiers in bed with a high fever or recovering from bronchitis. She panted in the half-light of hot and humid summer dawns in Martinique. In Brazil, unable to sleep in her sweltering hotel room, she spent a whole night wandering in the steamy streets of a rundown part of Rio, walking a few steps, then collapsing on a stoop or a low wall to catch her breath. A man she didn't know came to her in a flurry of Portuguese words, and as she wasn't able to answer him, stayed with her and held her hand, mute, helpless.

There is in her an opacity of the body, soft and white, contrasting with the intense luminosity of the face and the hands on which the skin, powdered white, still remarkably tight, becomes translucent, Japanese rice paper diffusing fire from within. The lips red, the eyebrows thick, the eyes fiery. The hair, dark and shiny curls touched with silver.

From across the table, Julian watches the play of her fingers, her face glowing above the *femme fatale*'s black, black from neck to feet, covering her.

She catches him looking at her. He has the eyes of a perverse and cunning teenager who still holds onto his androgynous status, a nonchalance in his figure and his clothes which arouses in her a powerful and ambiguous desire. One more time she's acutely aware of the age difference between them. He could be her son, as they say. Almost. And as usual her mother's ghost appears at her shoulder. It strongly disapproves of such unnatural coupling. It whispers, no lipstick, you look like a whore! If you must have makeup, make it light. Study! the familiar figure yells in her ear. You need an education, later a job. It's not in wearing skimmers and showing off your armpits that you're going to make it in life. She looked for sensuality between her parents. Their bed was forbidden to her. Never seen their thighs, the hair at the bottom of Daddy's belly. His penis, even little, casually dripping against the side of the toilet bowl. Did Daddy have a penis? Did he put it in Mummy? In her . . . ? Never such thoughts, never so sinful so . . . never words so . . . She talked in low tones with her best friend in the yard. Are you still a virgin? How does one make love? But how exactly? What the girl does, what the boy does. She refrained for a long time from finding out for herself. Her body swelled with curiosity, with desire that filled her whole. The Question in suspense. The mystery she was obliged to incarnate, harnessed with the feminine accoutrement. The bra straps, the suspender belt, the stockings twisting, growing ladders, the sanitary napkins crusted, the slip threatening to show. Signs of femininity were seething below the surface, which one had to do one's best to deny outwardly. That they might make their way to the outside was unthinkable.

Let's get out of here, she says to Julian, passing his suggestion of dessert. She likes to make her move first. To let them choose, to wait, would make her too vulnerable.

When desire springs in her, lavas penetrate organs, veins, muscles, roll down paths of skin tissues usually controlled by soldiers permanently at attention. The guards collapse, tongues of fire crackle, fly through the body in suspense, arouse nerves and senses. She catches a whiff of her own perfume on her wrist. Earlier she enjoyed the tender texture of a *quenelle de brochet,* then the sugary tartness of the black-currant sauce playing against the heavy and gamey richness of a pheasant. She drinks too much, small glasses half-filled with good Burgundy, its deep ruby rippling like watered silk. A bit drunk, she leans toward Julian. Okay? She feels like a vessel overflowing with voluptuous Oriental silks, spices and coffee majestically sailing upon his roused waters. Okay?

His pale eyes are lost in hers, widened by deep dark shadows. Their hands clasp each other among the stemmed glasses, above the silvery bread basket of an establishment that thinks quite well of itself. Mute, at a distance, their lips plunge at the same time in their wine.

Julian is reading his poetry again, this time languidly stretched on Salvine's bed. Salvine listens attentively, propped on one elbow. Darling, she says when he's finished. I don't know anything about poetry, even though I was quite a fan of Verlaine when I was growing up in Poitiers, but isn't this awfully overwritten? For you, I mean. I think you create better art with your life . . .

He shrugs. Drops the notebook angrily, turns away from her to face the window.

She wraps her arm around his waist, squeezing his balls, pulling him toward her.

. . . or with your body, for that matter.

Their bodies moving slowly, voluptuously against each other, they are barely aware of the blue lacquered walls, the edge of the mattress they hit with their shins and elbows, the smell of daffodils in a vase of lavender *pâte-de-verre,* the pink-grey of dawn washing out the light from the night-table lamp to a pale glow. These fragments of hard reality they are vaguely aware of flush their desire, giving it a heightened sharpness. Like all lovers, they are making love with their imagination. The distance in age and interests creates a void between them in which their desire surges.

In the morning she worries silently about circles under her eyes, afraid to look ten years older. She quickly slips into the bathroom without giving him time to hold her back.

He is beautiful. Young and all the perfection of body and skin. Above his temple stands one spike of hair, stubborn, which had been carefully combed back with gel in the evening. He looks for his cigarettes. She finds them on the floor, in the jumble of sheets, and lights one up, before slipping it between his lips, as she used to do when she had made love with a boy for the first time. She can't help stroking the tuft of unkempt hair. He flattens it, embarrassed, thinking how he used to be teased at school for this oddly placed strand.

He buries his face between her breasts in the opening of the robe. The movement bothers her, as well as the cliché that immediately presents itself: the matron revered by a mother-deprived adolescent. Eager to dissipate the image she gets up quickly and offers to make coffee.

Salvine's penthouse is so high up, approaching a window gives you vertigo. Julian always feels like a bird soaring toward Central Park, the other buildings surrounding the park tilted and distorted as if seen through a camera's fish-eye lense. In full daylight, even a grey late morning like this one which dulls the colors, the baroque apartment with its heavy Oriental carpets, its faux lapis lazuli or faux malachite walls, its rich paisley chintzes on the pillows and couches, its deep recesses and alcoves hung with dark brocades and crystal chandeliers like jewelry boxes glittering with precious stones, becomes a strange treasure vault flying above the city.

You should keep your curtains permanently drawn, Julian tells Salvine when he joins her in the kitchen, struggling with the cappuccino machine.

Why?

Because the intrusion of the city and of nature is a shocking contrast to the feeling one has at night of being inside a womb. A place like this shouldn't even have windows. It should be reached only after miles of subterranean passages. It should be in a castle sunk underwater with the whole Atlantis continent.

Then there would be a lot of little lively crustacea stuck like leeches to the furniture and the walls. Talk about nature!

It should be under Central Park, reached by mossy slippery steps.

Do you see me as a mermaid?

Maybe.

I am a Pisces, you know.

So? Know what I mean?

I like that contrast. I see this place as a rococo flying saucer drifting through space. Who said space vessels should be high tech and smooth and cold with Formica surfaces? And anyway space is the element to explore in the Age of Aquarius, the equivalent of sea for the Renaissance. Hold on a sec.

The phone is ringing. Salvine picks it up from a wall painted with a romantic vista of an English garden as seen from a belvedere, with birds chirping in the trees and a pond in the distance where a young fawn is drinking. The painted scene, a stunning trompe l'oeil, covers three walls of the kitchen, with different perspectives of the same garden, giving the viewer the illusion of standing at the center of the belvedere.

Yes, Salvine says. The ad in the *Village Voice*. Are you French? You sure don't sound it. How long have you lived here? Oh really? *Oui, je suis française moi aussi*. What? *Oh, c'est une longue histoire*. Why don't you come over here. I'll tell you about my research. She suggests a date and gives her address, jotting down the time on a pad.

What research are you doing, Julian asks. I didn't know you were doing any work?

Do I hear sarcasm in this sweet voice? But my dear, how do you suppose I made this money? Her hand sweeps through the kitchen toward the rest of the apartment. It was hard work, you know.

What? Being married to a millionaire?

Hey, it takes skills. Keeping men so happy they will cover you with presents and leave you their fortune when they die is an art that is almost lost. She hands him a cup of frothy coffee and pulls out warm croissants from the microwave oven. Men are getting better at it than women, she adds, giving Julian a sharp look.

1958.
Poitiers,
France

A couple embraces in a shabby hotel room. He is naked. She is wearing a peach-colored slip that he lifts above her hips. They don't talk. He is strong and well-built, with rough hands, the hands of someone who depends on them for a living. But he is a city man, not a peasant, maybe a truck driver or a construction worker. The line of the woman's back and hips and the man's hands are reflected by the oval mirror of a vanity across from the bed. Neither of them is aware of the reflection in the mirror. They are too busy groping for each other, grasping patches of skin, hanging onto fragments of lips, buttocks, shoulders. Their passion is all-consuming. They see each other so rarely and for such a brief time when they do that there is no space for distance between them, for the memory of other skins and other orgasms, for the consciousness of noises and shapes, for speech. They embrace avidly, their bodies twist, they roll among the clothes they didn't take the time to push away. They bite each other's necks like young bulls. When they are finished the man speaks. He is lying on his back, arms crossed behind his head. She is on her stomach, leaning on her elbows, her chin inside her palms. She doesn't look at him. You and me, he says. You and me . . . She turns around, presses her belly against his side.

I'm going to leave, she says.

He jumps. What time is it?

No. I mean leave. Really go. Get out of here. Leave this city. Leave everything.

He turns around, astounded.

What?

I don't like it here. It's not good for me. I don't want to end up in this town, married, with kids and a drunk husband like my mother.

Where do you want to go, Paris?

She runs her hand through her short hair, then makes a vague gesture, suggesting some faraway place. She sits up cross-legged, the peach slip chastely covering her breasts but tucked up high on her thighs. He stares at the place where the fabric curls on her flesh, but something in her attitude, proud, distant, stops him from thrusting his hand between her legs as if he owned them.

I don't know. Somewhere else. Martinique maybe. America.

What about me?

You . . .

He sits up too.

Yes. Me. Us.

He faces her.

How can you, now . . .

She takes his hands, appeasing.

I didn't say I was going to leave right away.

He pulls his hands out of hers, sticking them threateningly on his knees.

But why now? What . . .

Precisely, now. It's you. You gave me the taste of something else. Your comings and goings, your absence. I've felt the void, when you're not here.

It's because I'm not here often enough. He hits the pillow with his fists. But what do you want me to do, with the kind of job I have! You can't ask me to quit! I like the road. Ah! Women are all the same! But admit it, that you want to get married, to rent an apartment . . .

He gets up, grabs one bar of the brass bed with both his hands. She looks at him, incredulous. Her nape is fragile above her solid shoulders.

Well, I'm going to surprise you. After all, I don't give a fuck. I want you. You are more important than anything else for me. Even than my job. What do I care really! So? Is that what you wanted to hear?

She turns very cold.

You didn't understand. I'm not trying to get you. I don't care. I don't want to get married. You opened a door for me, don't you understand? No you don't, obviously. Okay. With you, it's alive, it's powerful, it makes me want to live, to live something else than what I have here.

He is still holding onto the bed, like a prisoner to his bars.

But not with me . . .

I don't know. We never talked about that.

And you don't think about it now! It doesn't even cross your mind!

Don't yell.

But he's breaking loose.

Okay. You want us to leave together? Where to? Paris? The Eiffel Tower? Drink wine at the well? We'll press grapes together, tread them under our feet. We'll get high on Alpine snow. No? You want the world? Here goes California, Mexico! At your feet, ma'm. We'll visit the Aztecs, walk up the pyramids. We'll touch the Pacific with our toes. We'll go get burned by the Acapulco sun, fuck on the banks of the Amazon. We'll go listen to Big Ben in London, cruise the Caribbean, row the Venetian canals, climb up the Parthenon in Rome . . .

In Athens.

What?

The Parthenon's in Athens.

He lifts up his arms. All right. In Athens. What does it matter? That's not what you want? But what the hell do you want?

She gets up slowly, puts on her stockings, her dress, her shoes, looks for her coat. He picks up her purse, holds it against him to keep her from leaving.

You don't get it. I don't know if I want to travel with you. I don't even know if I want to travel, like a tourist. I want to find out other things.

Alone.

He's spoken in a very low voice.

What's that?

Without me!

I don't know. Yes. Alone.

She's at the door, her back against the wall.

Give me my purse.

He moves toward her.

But I love you.

I love you, she breathes.

He takes her in his arms, the purse slips between them. He looks for some skin not yet covered by clothes, he touches her cheeks, her neck, her hair. He whispers I love you, I love you. She presses her lips against his, her whole body. Then she breaks the embrace, picks up her purse. He moans. No, don't go yet! Gently she opens the door and walks out, leaving it open. He collapses on the bed, his head in his hands. The oval mirror reflects the curve of his shoulders, his furrowed nape and the sheets in disarray around him.

The coquelicot candies

See, Salvine says, smoothing the large black-and-white print with her fingers. This is me in Poitiers before I came to the States. I was twenty.

Who's the guy? Lulu asks.

Salvine looks at the photo for a moment. He had taken it one of the last times they'd met in the hotel room, always the same room at the back of the hotel, opening on a little closed-in garden with a stone fountain. He had shot the mirror on the vanity, catching them both, him with the camera covering his eyes. That was the way he had devised to get the two of them in one photo.

A man I was in love with.

Very clever, says Lulu.

What?

The photo. The way he took it.

Yeah.

What happened? He dropped you?

Him? No, never. I left him. I couldn't stand . . . It felt like a trap. Poitiers was a trap. He made me realize that. The way he was. I realized I'd better get out of there quick if I wanted to do something with my life.

I like the slip you were wearing.

It had this very pretty flesh-pink. A lot of lingerie was that color, then.

I would have liked it.

It would have looked good on you. When I first saw you I thought you looked a little like me when I was your age. Except the hair color, of course.

From the windows of Salvine's living room overlooking Central Park the glitter of the city is dizzying. The Empire State Building tilts as Lulu stands up. In the dark the glass panes vanish. One more step and she walks in the dazzling lights. She flies in outer space. She squats down on the thick carpet, next to the void, far enough not to touch the glass, pretending it's not there.

Have you ever seen flying saucers? I wonder if there are space-ships gliding silently, at night, between the skyscrapers.

Spaceships are not silent, you know, Salvine says, standing next to Lulu, watching the city.

Why not? With modern technology. Can you see the sunrise from here?

From over there. Sometimes I watch it rise. An orange bowl in a light pink sky. I don't sleep very much these days. I love New York dawns in the summertime.

You shouldn't turn the light on at night. Not even candles for dinner. Instead the Empire State Building blinking away.

Why does everybody tell me what to do here?

I don't come uptown very often, Lulu says.

No. I wouldn't think so.

Salvine is not a writer. She is a rich woman with a past that she keeps to herself, because in the days when she was young there were certain things that a woman didn't do. Like traveling around

47

the world and sleeping around with men and living by her wits. She met a rich man when she was hanging out in Greenwich Village and was getting tired of it. He fell head over heels for her and married her. At that time she was at the height of her beauty. Sassy and fiery and wild like a blood mare. People said she married him for his money. It was not exactly true. She needed the security of money. Was always attracted to it. She had no taste for poverty. Even bohemian poverty. She used to say, you've got to come from the middle class to enjoy bohemian poverty. His family hated her. This Frenchwoman who looked men in the eye and wore clothes of dubious taste and overdid the jewelry and the perfume. They were Wasp and very proper, old money, a house on Nantucket. She thought they were a riot. When he smashed his Mercedes on the Massachusetts Turnpike going a hundred miles an hour they all stopped talking to her. Lucky for her it was an accident and she was in the Bahamas at the time, they would've gladly pinned a murder on her. Not his mother, though. His mother liked her. Curiously. She thought she was good for him. Salvine still goes and visits her. After ten years.

Salvine sends for two hamburgers with a double order of pickles and opens a bottle of Beaujolais. She says, I can't eat meat, even a hamburger, without opening a bottle of red wine and I can't finish a meal without a slice of good cheese. I suppose that means I'm still French.

Lulu can't figure out what Salvine wants from her. She says she interviewed other girls but so far Lulu is the only one she is curious about. She says, if I hear you talk, maybe I can understand who I am. But she doesn't seem to be the introspective type.

I want to understand, Salvine repeats.

What?

About changing culture, what it does to your memories, to your past.

Are you going to tape the interviews? Because I wouldn't be comfortable.

You can write too, if you want. Just notes, bits and pieces of memories. Drawings of objects.

Objects?

Yes, like this box of *coquelicot* candies, there.

She picks up a round metal can printed with coral-colored octagonal shapes, alternatively saying *Prenez du coquelicot* or *John Tavernier*. In front of the box the words

BONBONS COQUELICOTS

JOHN TAVERNIER

250 GRS. NET

are printed in blue on an eggshell background.

Have you ever had *coquelicots?* No? Do you know what they are? Small octagonal candies, poppy-red and terribly sweet. I can't offer you any. This box hasn't had *coquelicots* in it for decades. She shakes it for a moment. It sounds like it does, though, doesn't it? It's got paper clips in it. In Poitiers, Monsieur le Curé used to give the kids a *coquelicot* after Mass. He'd keep the same can as this in his Presbytère and would make the bonbons click in it just like that. Then he'd give one to each kid and when we were finished our tongues were bright red. Every time I shake this, whole Sundays in Poitiers come back to me.

Sort of like Proust's *madeleine?*

Right.

Lulu asks for coffee and Salvine comes back with two cups of cappuccino from the kitchen.

Lulu says she keeps a journal about certain things. In a way it's funny, or it's fate that she and Salvine met, because she writes about these events, these moments in her past. She doesn't know why. They kind of come to her. Like dreams, or nightmares.

Salvine leans toward her. Anecdotes, family scenes?

I guess just memories. Everybody has them. I just write them down. I don't like to show them. People don't understand.

You can tell me only what you want. It would be like, you know, friends exchanging, talking about their lives.

Lulu sips her coffee in silence, looking at the wall of windows.

Think about it, Salvine says. If you're interested. We can meet here whenever you want.

Are you going to write a book with that?

I don't know what I'm going to do. It's just an idea I had.

The memories have come back to me recently, Lulu says. When I first got here, it was as if I had no past. I dropped my French accent. I forgot everything. It was like being a blank page. Then little by little the dreams started to come.

Nunchaku

Lulu is moving through a sea of old clothes piled in a huge warehouse, thousands of square feet of them flattened out like cars on the scrap heap. They come apart with a sound of Velcro. The piles are high, they tower over her. She walks between them as if at the bottom of a dark canyon. A dusty light gleams from the windows at the far end of the loft, where a powerful machine fashions cubes of crushed material out of loose clothes.

She spots something white with black polka dots in the middle of a pile, and starts pulling at it.

Lady, you'll never get it that way, says a tall black attendant who's wheeling a cart in front of him. His voice is that of a white man and it becomes quirky like Raphael's as he moves the cart next to the block of clothes. The cart's got two metal arms that he slips along the polka-dot fabric to separate it from the rest of the pile, but instead they move on Lulu, prying her legs open. Then the levers turn into Raphael's arms struggling with her on her unmade bed. Please, let me, he says, please! She rolls over on her side, clutching her knees together: Leave me alone, she moans. Ask anything, anything else. I'll wear silk underwear and shave my pubic hair. I'll massage you until you yell out in pain, crying for mercy . . .

Raphael gets up, he pulls his silver belt out of his pants, swings it swiftly into the air, but misses the sharp hissing sound he attempted and throws it angrily across the floor.

Lulu woke up in a sweat, trying to kick his ghost away. The early morning light came through whitish in the small bedroom. Raindrops were hanging like crystals from the window bars. The sky washed out after the night rain.

He always came to her in the dead of night. His spirit haunted her dreams, even though she rarely thought of him during her waking hours, at work, or alone in the evenings, slowly chewing her food, a paperback propped behind her plate. His face rarely appeared to her. He was a voice, and a succession of quick moves, somewhat like a boxer's jabs.

The ceiling collapsed today in the Journal Square station in New Jersey. It was a ceiling of tile and reinforced plaster. Two people died in the accident. The radio in the cab also said there would be a high in the mid to upper nineties, possibly a record high of one hundred, and Raphael started to feel his skin get sticky.

One more step and he'd have fallen down the empty elevator cage seven stories below. His legs turned soft as jelly, his heart tightened. One more step and that was it. His name but a vague memory. One moment alive and well, the next gone. As fast as the snap of a finger. Smashed at the bottom, skull exploded, splashed with blood. *A quoi tient la vie.* He went on chatting casually with the woman, his tongue on automatic pilot, independent from his brain. Later, walking safely on the sidewalk, looking three times each way before crossing the streets, he thought, she could've pushed me. Just a little shove. Not much strength needed. Even a small woman like her, chest like a teenager's and skinny thighs, frail-boned. No problem. Coming up to him, pretending to show him something. Look. Her hand on his shoulder. A little flirtatious maybe. Bring his resistance down. What resistance? He probably wouldn't have had any. He doesn't even know the woman, for God's sake. Just met her downstairs. Rode the elevator up with her to show her his aqua green '66 Chevy trimmed with rhinestones and shimmering mermaids rising from the fins, abruptly decided against selling it and asked for an outrageous price, higher than the ad stated. Said he'd thought better of it. She looked surprised and he wanted to kiss her real bad, so he put his hand on her knee as they sat side by side on the front seat, examining the dashboard. When they got out of the car and walked to the elevator he didn't pay attention, he was looking at the curve of her upper lip, he would've walked straight into the void . . . Then he realized where he was and stopped dead in his tracks, a foot maybe from the edge of the empty cage, and called down the hole for the elevator man. She could've leaned slightly on him, pointing to something, him moving one step forward, and in the split second of his imbalance . . . Her strength would be purely mental. Sheer will power. Focused on her open palm resting on the ripped shoulder seam of his T-shirt. All her mental powers concentrated on that spot. Holding her breath, the energy flowing to her hand, a formidable impulse as if getting ready for the high jump at the Olympics, her eyes going black. Then the shove. He wouldn't know it was happening. It might even be a high, ultimate fear twisting the bowels, heart jumping in the throat like on a roller-coaster ride, except it would be for real. Does the body know the difference?

What's the matter with you, the new woman in his life asked when Raphael stopped at her place on the way back. You look upset.

He shook his head.

Just thinking.

Did you sell the car?

He shook his head no, and pulled out a nunchaku from his bag, its two handles made of well-worn dark walnut, held by a rusty chain.

53

From Japan, he said. My friend had it shipped especially for me. It's an antique. He lightly stroked the smooth wood. Then he whipped the sticks out. They unfurled threateningly. Did you know this was originally used for beating rice?

She looked at him with a silent smile, the kind he hated, he thought was superior, sneering.

Another weapon for your collection?

He shrugged, whipped the chucks again through the air. They zigzagged sharply, the loose stick lashing straight out. He juggled them a few times with quick sharp moves of his wrist. The nunchaku clicked and hissed. An angry snake going after its prey, tongue darting and hissing. He circled his girlfriend, lashing out at her from a distance, going for the kill.

You're looking pretty mean for a rice-beater, she said, stretched out on her couch. And he thought maybe it was time to look around for a new girl.

Raphael had a collection of photos around his house, of ex- or current girlfriends. Big prints mounted on cardboard hanging on the walls, snapshots and Polaroids tacked above his desk, propped against the edges of books on his shelves, a sepia-colored one, framed, under glass, leaning on a gilded bookrest tucked in a corner of his fireplace. There were blonds and redheads—he was especially fond of redheads, thought they were more sensual, but wouldn't be convinced until he was satisfied their pubic hair was of the authentic color—brunettes, black and South American girls, close-ups taken with his Nikon, medium shots down to the waist, some with him taken with the timer or by a friend. Memories, he said. I can't part with any of them. More like a hunting bag, Lulu thought. But after they stopped sleeping together she didn't ask him to take hers down. She gave him the benefit of the doubt. She looked beautiful and mysterious in it, a good image to pass on to posterity, she thought. Last time she visited him it wasn't anywhere in sight. My main squeeze got jealous, he said, trying to pass an arm around her waist. She has pretty good taste, don't you think? Fuck you, she said.

. . .

54

Now he is working on his chaku sticks again, practicing his wrist rotation.

Lulu looks at the flowers growing in the window boxes and on the fire escapes, clay pots in tight rows on the metal stairs, blocking the passage in case of fire. They make her think of an Arab garden. In the shade of the high walls covered with shiny leaves and faded blue flowers, a clear jet of water springs out of a stone fountain, light, cool drops splashing in scorching-hot afternoons. Mats on the marble floor, pillows thrown on the mats. And women lying about, their long cotton robes rolled up on their knees, their round shoulders.

Why does New York always appear to her as Third World visions? These smells of rot, these overbloomed flowers hanging from the wire fences enclosing the vacant lots. Bright-colored murals, sensual brown lips, small children running down the street, teenagers playing baseball in the dust, women joking from the stoops, their hands on their wide hips . . . graffiti of fire, angry blacks, sharp, angular lines rising on metal doors and freshly painted walls, like a signature from hell.

I want you, said Raphael's eyes, turquoise blue like a Florida swimming pool. They were pressed elbow-to-elbow in an overcrowded bar. The eyes also said he was drunk. But dead sober in his desire for her.

She had met him once before, but hadn't paid much attention to him. He was a guy with a good sense of humor. Warm. Quirky voice. Sexual. But not for her, she'd thought. Why? She could only think of one reason: receding hairline. And yet. Now she wanted to touch his crotch; slide her hand down his thighs, tight in worn blue jeans, a metal belt loose around his hips. His voice broke when it rose too high, it had a strange effect on her, and she leaned toward him, searching for his mouth.

Things started to go downhill for them when he decided he wanted to fuck her in the ass. It hurt like hell, no matter how they were doing it, the pain didn't turn her on like he said it would. What he said in substance was: suffer, and you'll see Nirvana, a very Catholic argument in her opinion. But the pain didn't turn her on, as far back as she remembered no pain ever turned her on. Shoving himself against her backside, he told her there was something wrong with her, that she wasn't sensual, that she didn't know what was good for her, that she was uptight, middle class, frigid. She was scared to lose him, or did she want to show him how adventurous she was sexually—she'd rise to any challenge? Anyway she did her best. They went through jars of Vaseline and tubes of K-Y jelly. She did it on the side, on all fours, on the back, legs up, offering her rear end to his blessings. But first she made him wait, kept him panting, offered alternatives, promised anything he wanted. Finally she went through it, her teeth set, practicing her yoga deep breathing. When it was over with, she was relieved. It bought her a week of freedom. There was a tacit agreement between them that he would give her a few days' rest between sessions.

In the past fear could vanish while she was drinking a glass of creamy milk, so thick it tasted like light whipped Chantilly. It would flow down her throat like a silk ribbon. At three, fear could be forgotten, just by running through a field speckled with buttercups and daisies, arms wide open, laughing, soft lips circled up on little wolf's milky teeth.

When Raphael moved around, paced the living room, Lulu felt as if he was sitting on her chest, her throat choked, and nothing could ease the pressure. He talked about his brother, he talked about some sausages, left over unwrapped in the fridge, that would go bad, he talked about his job, someone he worked with who was trying to give him trouble, get in his way. He was persuasive, he seemed to be trying to convince her, striking argument after argument against her silence, her evasive answers. Then she got caught, or challenged, and argued back. Soon they were locked in their respective roles, he on the offensive, she on the defensive. She felt cornered. She was actually squeezed at the end of the sofa, her back slightly hunched. She was vaguely aware of her jaw tightening, her breathing getting short. She used irony, mocked him, he attacked back. They resumed their argument at the dinner table. There was a friend with them. A girlfriend of Lulu's. She tried to steer the conversation away from whatever it was they fought about, his job this time, but they kept going back to it. You know what, Lulu finally said, her heart beating in her throat. She sat up in her chair and leaned over the table, her plate a mess of barely touched steak coagulating in its bloody juice and soggy French fries, you think you're so cool, but you know what you are? A ridiculous, pompous jerk with a diminutive organ.

What!?

You make me want to puke.

He moved fast. The red wine splashed up in a fast arc from his stemmed glass to her face. It dripped over the marble tabletop and the salt-and-pepper shakers and on the edges of the plates.

Shit, Lulu said, standing up, wiping her face with her napkin. And she retreated to the bathroom where she sobbed behind the locked door.

Later her friend told her, I can't believe you didn't throw your glass right back at him. Don't worry, Lulu said, I'll get back at him, and she took two lovers, one whom she brought over for dinner at their place several times, the other one she took to parties all over town.

Raphael had the most limpid eyes and a lanky body and he read her Antonin Artaud late at night. She showed him her diary once and he sneered. She had moved in with him. It was understood they could both have lovers. When they made love, he made her come telling her what he did in bed with his other girlfriends.

Then the wine splashed red in her face, the taste of it lingering over her lips.

She didn't keep the two lovers very long. It was too much trouble. Instead she dropped Raphael. Moved on with her life.

Now he's become a filmmaker. She reads about him in the

papers. When they see each other, he touches her around the waist or on her bare shoulders and she shudders.

They meet in the street, Raphael offers to take her for a ride in his old Chevy, the one he decorated with mermaids and costume jewelry. They ride up the freight elevator to the seventh floor where he keeps it parked. But the car is nowhere in sight, they look all over for the green plastic sheet that covers it up. They walk forever it seems on the huge parking-lot floor, then they go toward the elevator to call the attendant. Raphael's agitated, he's not paying attention, she sees him walking straight up to the edge of the empty cage, on impulse she grabs him by the shoulder, startled he shakes his arm, grabs her by the wrist. She loses her balance, they're holding onto each other, their feet dance at the very edge, she feels her rubber sole slide right down the metal ledge. No! she screams. She's hanging on to him for dear life . . . She won't let him . . . She's going down. She won't let him get away. Her nails bite sharp as needles around his wrist. She feels him teeter. Their screams echo down the chute, seven stories to their death.

No! Lulu yelled, eyes wide open in the pearl-white dawn glistening through the Japanese shade, struggling among the sheets at the foot of her bed.

I'm tired of your little games, the new woman in his life said, sitting up naked on the side of his bed, after Raphael attempted to describe his new conquest to her. I've had it. Good-bye. She got dressed swiftly and slammed the door behind her, scurrying, her sandal straps undone and dangling around her ankles.

Alone, Raphael grabbed the handle of his Japanese nunchaku, and cracked a perfect arc. He sighed, wondered if it was too late to call the girl he met at a party the day before, decided against it and stretched on his back, arms folded across his eyes, his torso and legs and whole body tight as a corpse slipping into rigor mortis.

Betrayal

Lulu's unsent letter to her former boyfriend, Raphael.

Raphael dear,

Because I never said that I felt betrayed, do you think I forgot? It seems so far anyway now, years and several lovers away, you know I tried to erase the past, except one never does of course, as you used to tell me. I think sometimes, living in New York, I have become hard as stone, which terrifies me, because I wonder if I've lost myself again. My legs wobbled under me when I tried to do anything as public as trying to cross the schoolyard, or standing in the middle of the living room talking to a guest. My stomach, my liver, my intestines had sunk like rocks in the frozen sea of my liquids and spleen, my limbs obeyed outside commands, puppets whose strings were pulled by various voices giving contradictory orders. It resulted in a near-paralysis of my brain. If the paralysis had been total, I guess I would have lucked out, but where outside control had not completely taken over, I was screaming anxiety. An exposed wound purulent with screwed-up thoughts, high paranoia, intense jealousy, feelings of abandonment and the vertigo that seized me when the wound burst open (remember how I had height fright?). It still happens: I topple into the abyss, but so slowly I seem to be immobile, or maybe what's so freaky is that nothing holds anymore, it's a void, no gravity, the heart spins, the void is inside of me, spiraling out at high speed, the blackness spreads, it's a feeling of having been torn apart, of only existing in the fall, the only moment when the self actually experiences power (the puppet having had its strings cut off), but it's a power of chaos, or a chaotic power, a mind/body/soul disjointed and in awe of each other, and in a long silent scream, the whole of my energy focused to avoid the irreparable split, I strive to recall—but it's a long lost elusive dream, like trying to recapture the feeling of a hot beach in summertime when you shiver half-naked in a snow storm—the short-lived ecstasy of harmony.

But I digress. Or maybe not. Maybe your betrayal was nothing else than the reopening of the wound, a confirmation of my nonexistence, having let myself be erased by you for a whole night, and then by a string of days and nights. I had given myself over to you, strings and all, you were holding me together, but it was my doing, I know, I am not accusing you of having taken me over, even though, as little aware as you were of that dependence, you enjoyed it, and at times also, to be honest, you resented it, you resented not to feel the pull coming from me, the contrary force, it was too slack and it intrigued you, then you pulled harder to make sure. Maybe that night when you finally fucked H., fucked her with your eyes, right in front of me at dinner, then took her to our room while I waited in the dark listening to every creak coming from upstairs, maybe that night you just pulled harder. To see how far you could go. Maybe I was your dream come true. Maybe you could go too far and not be punished by it. Like a kid pushing his limits. The metaphor is seductive, but not quite right because I am the one who started it all. Because in truth I had already fallen out of love before you even so much as looked at another girl. Because I am the one who took a lover first.

You said you didn't mind of course. You were supposed to be a free spirit, a child of your time, in favor of free love and nonpossessiveness. Jealousy, you said, was a bourgeois sentiment, betrayed a hopeless middle-class hang-up on propriety. I froze when you spoke like that. I waited, trembling, for the blade to fall on my neck. Meanwhile you practiced delicate tortures. You remember this girl on the beach in North Carolina, I forget her name, but never her eyes, they were of that blue about which people say, did you see the color of her eyes but they can't really tell what it is. Lavender or violet, truly rare, and her milky skin, and her hair long, straight and black with thick bangs stroking her eyelids, sensual lips, and skinny thighs, she could've been a model, why wasn't she a model? I remember her hands distinctly, they were bony and she chewed her fingernails. She wore a short see-through blouse of white Indian cotton and no bra of course. Writing about her my mouth waters. I wonder, how could you have resisted her at all? Your eyes never left her. You sat next to her in cafés, drove her around in somebody's battered Jeep. All the guys were after her. I wanted her too. You didn't do a thing with her, you said, but I spent my nights lying flat on my back while you got hard for her, then you asked me to turn around and you took me from behind, telling me how sexy you thought she was. She was somebody's girlfriend's best friend. She was AVAILABLE. The trouble for you is that she was also loyal to women, a concept that, somehow, didn't fit into your unbourgeois notion of the world. Until she came one night . . . But let me not anticipate. I am the one who started it all you said.

I tried to forget you, but I see your face everywhere. You seem to be the darling of women's magazines. I can't open a magazine that I don't see your aquamarine eyes and confident smile, as befits one of the hot up-and-coming filmmakers of your generation, tortoiseshell glasses, grey cashmere turtleneck. There're dark shadows under your eyes now, the smile lines around your mouth have deepened, you're getting to be quite bald, I can read your age on these photos and it reminds me you are ten years older than me.

They say one forgives with time. But you know what, Raphael? I look at the sexy smile and I want to wipe it off the page. I look at these blue eyes and I see tiny daggers piercing the small irises of glossy paper. I've made a doll in clay. I dressed it up with Ken clothes. I traced the eyes blue and a fine line around them to make the tortoiseshell glasses and I stuck red-hot needles in it. I burned cow-dung in front of it, let it bathe in the foul fumes. Your face still shows up in the glossies. But just you wait, Raphael. I know it's only a matter of time.

The Chrysler
Building

Mystique is late for the show. She runs, zigzags between the kids playing basketball against the wall of a building. She doesn't wait at the light, a cyclist shows up in front of her, motions to her to move forward. Too late, she's already stepped back. He circles around her, yells at her. Fucking lady! She yells back, go fuck yourself.

The club is dark. It's a cool, humid cave. The ceiling, the walls, are painted black. The lights come from pink spiral-shaped neons. There is the usual line along the bar waiting to get into the backroom.

Hurry up, says Chuck, the second barman, without lifting his eyes from the glass in which he is pouring a shot of whiskey. They're gonna start without you!

Shut up!

. . .

Mystique can't take it anymore. She does some warm-up exercises, lifts up a leg. Starts on one foot, rotates a hip. Ah shit! What are you gonna do now? She's got bubble gum stuck between two molars. She had bright red cheeks like lady apples when she was a little girl, she used to be embarrassed by them and hide them in her hands. And her chapped skin in winter.

She bends toward the mirror, touching her cheeks with her fingertips, talking to herself. God! Madame plays the coquette, paints her nails shell-pink, with canteloupe shades. I've always loved pink mixed with yellow. It's a sunny color. Have you ever thought of getting a tattoo? And I don't mean a heart pierced with an arrow, a snake, a *Mom I love you* spread on a biceps, but the elaborate and perverse work of art blooming on the kidneys, straddling a round hip, or an exquisite dragonfly ready to take off from a thin shoulder. She shrugs. Hers wouldn't work. They are on the voluptuous side. Ripe flesh. It must be age, she thinks, forgetting she has never been skinny. She lights a cigarette. In the mirror her hair is black at its root, bursting into bright yellow, spiked up toward the sky. Maybe it's time to change hairstyles. I am getting out of fashion. That's what she says at the end of each cycle. Last time was when she sported a thick entangled mane of hair matted into dreadlocks. Her reaction had been extreme. She had clipped it herself and finished the job with a razor blade. Clean-shaven. Her skull a bizarre baby-white. She had never realized how uneven a skull can be, the bumps and hollows at the wrong places. Well, okay, not all skulls. Not those perfect Nazi blond dolichocephalic skulls that make a racy profile. Hers was tender and fragile like a newborn chicken—a five-o'clock shadow after a few hours of smooth billiard ball.

A tough cookie. They aren't gonna get her. Why? Because they "got" her so many times before. In that distant past that, having been digested many times, has turned into legend. Then to a pale violet handwriting carefully traced between the pages of an old leather notebook.

We all start with smooth skin, limpid eyes, dazzling smile, plump cheeks, tender like cake. And then what? Maybe if you yell loud enough your scream will break the mirrors.

. . .

I wanted to come to New York, thinks Lulu, running toward the Blue Night. Wasn't it supposed to be the promised land? The wind blows straight into her face. Hot ocean wind knocking down the beer cans in the gutter. At least you can breathe here. Plenty of fresh air. Can't think straight, though. Pull yourself together. Take it easy. Man, I can't believe it. Will you please listen to me. They don't understand. It would be too dangerous. A monkey locked in his cage, nutty as a fruitcake, gnawing his nails to the quick. Me against me. There are quite a few people in her head—she wonders if it's what they call multiple personalities—whispering in her ears.

Ed shows up in the dressing room behind Lulu, pulling Mystique out of her reverie.

Action, he yells. C'mon.

Let them wait! That's what they're here for, right? They'll think I am even more special.

Mystique is doing a new number. She choreographed it herself, with approving nods from Marty sucking on his diamond ring. She runs with her pink satin high-heel slippers with black ostrich pom-poms. She does a pastiche of a classic cabaret number. Berlin 1930, she says. She doesn't know for sure and could care less. Berlin 1930. New York 1940. Paris 1920. She has but the vaguest idea of history, can't even remember other people's stories. Her legs are harnessed in black net stockings, she's got a siren's dress on with silver scales she smooths with the flat of her hand, fingers spread out on her hip, following the groin, like she saw Mae West do it.

The four of them move forward on the stage to salute, hand in hand. Bleached white hair, spiky with Dippity-doo. Juicy pussy, he said. And did you want me to . . . Echo. Me too too too. Their tiger-striped Spandex tights bulge below the fat of the buttocks. Keeping tight together. Black wraparound sun glasses, mysterious around the temples. Spiky pumps with murderous heels, mouth slashing across the face like a wound.

The dressing room smells of dirty feet, of the sweet odor of grass burned in a thin joint, passed, flattened out, between finger and thumb.

Hey, gimme the Coke, Lulu, fuzzy-head. And stop spitting in it!

I'm not spitting. I'm making lipstick juice.

Mystique spreads her clawlike nails to grab the Coke bottle.

Her waist is squeezed into a satin corset, her black jersey cut low on one side, high around the neck, tightened by a huge triangular metal clip with sharp edges. In her open-toe sandals, the polish on her nails is chipping.

Lulu is sitting at the makeup counter, smoking a Marlboro.

puking against a street lamp
you see the sky turn pink

sings Mystique, unhooking her corset. Mystique has rainbow hair tonight, shades from green to pink, and cosmic energy.

The swinging door opens with a kick, letting in six foot eight inch Ed, his body-builder's trunk trapped in a tight Lurex tank-top.

Mystique holds her corset up coyly with both hands, pretending to be prudish, and yells:

Hey, Ed, split, man! This is women's turf, here!

Hurry up, girls, he grumbles. We're closing early tonight. Remember the new schedule?

Nobody listens to him. Sirouelle and Andrée kiss in a corner, sitting on the floor in the middle of a heap of tissue-paper costumes.

Mystique's skin is wan without makeup, or maybe it is the contrast with the violent paint that she uses on her face that makes her seem so pale. It's like an underskin. Almost too intimate. She invites Lulu to her place after the show. They walk through the thick Saturday night crowd. They walk down the streets hollowed out with empty lots. In the light of the street lamps, Puerto Rican men are sitting on plastic chairs playing dominoes, the women and the girls settled on the nearby stoops bottle-feeding babies. Kids hanging out in clusters in front of the corner *bodegas,* kids walking to the hip-hop beat blasting out of their boxes.

Someone has painted Mystique's front stoop red. Long awkward blood-red trails that leave plaques of grey cement uncovered like leper's skin.

A rock 'n' roll song is blaring behind her door, she always leaves the radio on to keep the robbers away, and she runs to turn the sound down, kicks off her shoes, massages her toes.

Jesus! I'm getting corns with these shoes. Fucking brand new forty-dollar pumps! Do you want to drink something? I could die with this heat.

Lulu takes off her shoes too, walks barefoot toward the window.

Do you mind if I open it?

Go ahead. It's a fucking oven.

Mystique gets up to turn on the fan.

The Chrysler Building cuts through the foggy sky, its scales brightly lit.

It's my favorite skyscraper, Lulu says, pointing to the scales shining on top of the building. The first I went to visit when I came to New York.

How long have you lived here?

A few years.

Mystique doesn't ask more questions than necessary. She listens if she is spoken to. But she won't solicit information. If someone suggests she lacks basic human curiosity, she says life is no police cross-examination, and anyway, you don't get to know people by listening to them, but by looking at them, smelling them, sniffing them. Mystique is suspicious of the intellect. She only trusts her senses.

Lulu looks at New York and New York escapes her. Her eyes run, in panic. *Sauve qui peut.*

Beautiful Lulu, rose-bud-rose-*nanan,* rose-bud-*bonbon*-candy-*acidulé-de-vache.* Peppermint-candy-*à-la-menthe-poivrée poivrot* wino lying on the Bowery, unshaven, in front a cheap whiskey. Worlds/words slipping against each other.

Have you ever thought what the suburbs of a science-fiction city would look like? Lulu says. Apartments with old broken-down computers decorated with pink frilly knick-knacks dripping with tassels, Saint Christopher medals or Mickey Mouse stickers?

And microwave ovens serving as planters!

Elle est morte en couches

Your mother didn't die in giving birth to you. She was crazy. You understand. Nuts, nutsy. Cuckoo. They put her away. I guess they call it psychosis. She didn't die when you were born. She went crazy for good the day the Americans dropped the bomb on Nagasaki. Said things like it was the end of the world, the apocalypse. Poor thing, she was deranged.

But wait, it was in 1945. That's impossible, I was born thirteen years later.

Yes. She recovered for a while. She maintained herself on and off until you were born. But she couldn't handle a baby. She relapsed for good after the birth. I mean your birth. The birth had been very painful, my God, something like thirty hours of labor. She wanted to have a natural delivery, in those days it was called psychoprophylactic. But in spite of her preparation the pain was atrocious. After all this time she still wasn't dilating enough. And then she pushed and she pushed and you wouldn't come out, maybe she wanted to hold you back, so they used the

69

forceps and when that didn't work out they did a C-section but the anaesthetic wasn't well measured and she woke up screaming. She had loved being pregnant, she was very proud of her full belly, she was never that big, always a little thing, she loved it when men followed her in the street and whistled at her from behind, and when they caught up with her and saw her stomach she watched them blush, beg pardon, stutter, walk away embarrassed. She thought she looked beautiful and she was. Never saw a complexion like that. You think you've got nice skin, creamy, tight, you should've seen hers. Milk and roses we used to say in the family. Her face was like lit up from inside. It glowed. Men thought she was ravishing. But she was, what's the word, promiscuous? She had no morals, you know what I mean. A tramp. Believe me. There was something wrong in her head. She was crazy. It wasn't her fault.

That's not true. *Elle est morte en couches*. She died while giving birth to me.

No. That's what they told you. I'll always remember her back from the clinic with the baby wrapped up in a white blanket. She had wanted everything white. She didn't want blue in case it would be a girl, or pink in case it would be a boy. She was obsessed with white. She said babies incarnated purity. The baby—you—were dressed all in white, undershirt, cap, swaddling clothes. I saw her coming out of the car—it was a *Quinze,* a Citroën shiny black that belonged to our father. She was dressed in a white chiffon dress and had a white ribbon tied in her hair, and she was standing very stiff, the baby in her outstretched arms like an offering, or maybe she didn't know how to hold you, even though I doubt it, every mother, in her heart, knows how to hold a baby.

You're lying. She died just after I was born. Her heart failed her. I never even got a chance to be at her breast. *Elle est morte en couches.*

That's what they told you. They thought it would be easier for you to take than knowing your mummy was in a mental asylum. You would have wanted to visit her. It was too horrible. At the end she wet her bed.

It's not true.

Why don't you believe me?

Either you're lying now or you did then. Who's to say you were lying the first time?

We think you can handle the truth now.

We. Who's "we"?

She lived to be thirty-two. She died when you were at summer camp.

You see. You're lying. I never went to summer camp.

Well. Whatever you call it. That time when you went on vacation at that place, with all those kids.

Bruneau.

Yes. Bruneau. She was buried while you were away. It was very discreet. We didn't want you to know, or for anyone to tell you about it. It didn't make any difference after that. She was dead anyway.

Who's that, Salvine asks as Lulu turns off the tape recorder.

My aunt. My mother's sister. She raised me.

Did she know you recorded that conversation?

No. It was kind of an accident. I had been recording a tape, you know, some music, and she came in and we started talking, and when I realized that the tape recorder was still on, I just left it on. I thought it would be proof.

Of what?

Of her lies. I didn't trust her. She always lied to me. Especially about my mother. She kept rewriting history to suit her needs. But of course she denied it. I thought I was crazy, that I was imagining things. That I was hallucinating, like my mother. They drove her to it. I know.

Were you ever able to prove that your aunt lied to you?

No. I keep thinking maybe she was alive all that time.

Don't you think that if she had been alive she would have wanted to see you?

I don't know. Not if she was really crazy. All I know is that I have no memory of her. So I keep inventing her.

Scenes of
New York life
#9

The phone rings again. Lulu's in hiding. The answering machine picks up on the third ring, and Mystique's voice rolls on, mechanical. Lulu's asked her to tape the message for her. Her own voice, even disembodied, electronic, felt too vulnerable. Mystique doesn't announce herself nor Lulu, she just says flatly, if you want to leave a message, please do so after the beep. Impersonal. Long silence. Beep. The same voice drops the same message, the same for the last four days. It's Mario. I've got to speak to you. Urgent. And leaves a number. Each time a different number.

After the answering machine clicks off, Lulu checks the double bolt at the door, then that each window is shut tight. She walks in the dark, doesn't want to be an easy target moving backlit from window to window. From across the street or across the well the eye can plunge deep into the heart of her narrow railroad apartment. The only light is the white glare of the tv set alive with close-ups of Lauren Bacall in *To Have and Have Not*, nostrils flaring, eyes darting sideways like quick elegant butterflies, the long sweep of her hair shining silver on the screen, lips mouthing throaty words. Lulu gets back into bed, knees up to her navel, sheet pulled up, and watches hard, determined not to fall asleep.

The weather report wakes her up in the morning with the sun blazing in her face through the shades and she opens her eyes to a figure waving a long stick over a surreal map of the United States threatened by a mass of nasty dark clouds marching from the north country. She gets up and looks out the window, the fire escapes from the buildings across the street glitter like rare jewels in the morning sun.

Fuck, she says. It's barely dawn.

The phone rings and the machine comes on. Lulu turns up the sound. It's Mystique's voice. Couldn't be dawn. Time to get up, kid, she hears on the line. Lulu picks up the receiver. What time is it?

Eleven in the morning, Saturday the nineteenth. I wanted to invite you out for brunch. Unless you're busy, of course. Am I disturbing you?

No, Lulu says. I thought it was earlier, is all. Give me a half-hour, okay?

Mario's called again, Lulu says as they sit down in a small garden café flooded with sun. She puts on her black sunglasses and shades her back and arms with a flowered chemise. Mystique offers her naked face shiny with sunblock to the burning rays.

What's the point of exposing your skin to the sun if you're using sunblock? Lulu asks.

I like the heat, the feel of it.

Don't you think it might mess up your skin?

No. The whole idea is that it filters all the UV and what have you. But my skin is already messed up anyway. I found out too late about sun damage, and what do you think, there're miracle cures for aging? So what about Mario?

I've got four messages from him on my machine now. I don't erase them. Four days in a row. Each time he leaves a different phone number. He scares the shit out of me but I like his voice. I'm trying to explore the nuances of his vocal tones. He sounds Latin.

It figures, with his name. What are you scared about, exactly?

Why is he so persistent?

Who do you think he is?

A rapist. A killer. I don't know. I fantasize he calls me from across the street and observes all my moves. He's got a pair of binoculars and looks right into my place. He watches me from his window, watches me naked, watches me going to the bathroom, knows all about my schedule, my tastes in clothes, the expressions on my face, my moods, what I do when I am alone, what I don't do, the way I pick my nose, the way I wipe myself after I take a shit, if I masturbate, what I read. Can I borrow a cigarette? I turn off all the lights at night, keep only the tv light on. Why would he do that? What is he looking for? Biding his time, looking for the right time, find me defenseless? And then what?

Would a rapist call you, announce himself? I thought they'd just walk in your window from the blue, in the dead of night?

Bullshit. It's usually the lover you just turned down, his ego's crushed, he wants to get back at you. Or the guy with the acne scars down the hall you borrow sugar from when you're out of it.

They both sip their café au lait in the big white bowls. Lulu says they used to have bowls like that in her house when she was growing up, theirs were scalloped, decorated with red and blue rectangles. She says it's her favorite way to drink coffee, both hands cupped around the bowl, keeping warm. She says, Mystique, I am thinking of moving out. I am terrified.

And live where? How can you find another place that cheap? You're certainly welcome to stay at my place for a few days.

Maybe he has some kind of connection with Sarah, you know, the girl who's subletting me her apartment.

74

Where is she? Can you get hold of her?

She's in Europe for a year.

Why don't you call Mario back? Rather than stay passive and freak out each time he calls.

Would you do it with me?

Hold your hand and all that? Sure.

They call from the Blue Night before and after the show. They try the last number Mario has left and get a busy signal every time. Two of the other three numbers don't answer. Finally a woman's voice, bored, annoyed, comes on the line, rising slightly as she repeats Mario, Mario who? No, sorry, I don't know anyone with that name. Check your number.

Merde, Lulu says. Do you think he picks out numbers haphazardly from the phone book?

Out in the hot humid New York City night mixing into the crowd pulsing down the avenue, big boxes blasting from one end of a block to the other, vendors selling used LPs, secondhand clothes, shoes, hats, hardcovers of suspicious origin, antique plates and glasses, odd tea and coffee sets, curios, plastic and bead earrings, all spread flat on faded velvet or plaid fabrics along both sides of the sidewalk, the evening strollers threading their way in between, shops all opened, brilliantly lit, doing business, customers in and out, the flow running up and down Avenue A, Second Avenue, Saint Mark's Place, locals, beggars, bag ladies, bridge and tunnelers, uptowners slumming at Veselka, Odessa, long low shiny black and grey limos crouching double-parked, late openings around the square spilling deadpan chic groups with an attitude, drinking California champagne out of plastic tumblers on car hoods, moving off to side streets looking for the right people, not wanting to be seen hanging out with the anonymous, the uncool. Let's get out of this circus, Mystique says.

Tillie, the bag lady, is lying on a couch trashed in a vacant lot, her felt hat pushed down, a blanket pulled up to her eyes in spite of the heat. A quarter of a block down from her, the Poet gives his performance. Dressed in a suit jacket, a tie, a pair of shorts and his skinny naked legs sticking like rooster's feet out of laced-up black combat boots, the Poet has set up his box at a street corner and put on his pre-recorded monologues full blast. He's standing, his arms folded on his chest, repeating the words to himself, his eyes and his forehead tense under the horn-rimmed glasses, while listeners gather around him at a certain distance, listening respectfully. Tillie pulls her blanket farther up, covers her ears with it.

Why is it, Mystique asks, that we always have to pretend we are closer to our ideal than we really are. We all fall short of our own expectations (or is it others' expectations?). We all are more ambiguous, more sinful, more debauched, lazier, less committed, more homebodies than we'd like to admit.

Why do you say that? Lulu asks.

Just a thought.

Each big city distills its own poison. Paris, the grey city, cold slow rain slippery on wet greasy cobblestone streets, blasé bitchiness; New York, frantically narcissistic, shallow, hyperactive creativity. It may take awhile to feel the poison's effect, especially for a foreigner whose very foreignness is a strong antidote, until it gradually thins out, sometimes not for years. They say foreigners who move to Canada seem immune to the arctic winter for the first two or three years, because their bodies have stocks of vitamins A or D or E, or whatever it is that the sun provides, until their system wears off and they, too, see their skin breaking out, turning a yellowish color, and entertain thoughts of suicide in early April, due to the lack of sun during the long winter months.

In France, things were slow. Every step counted, had to be accounted for. Your past, your childhood, your parents' life, their childhood, their errors, their lapses, the memories of the wars, old conversations, declarations from half a century back, were carefully compiled, it was the baggage your childhood was harnessed with. It used up the better part of your brain, most of your emotional capacities, like a complicated software stocked on a single-drive diskette. It didn't leave much room to operate, bring in new data.

They end up in a bar on Houston and get drunk on gin and tonic, a silly way to get drunk, Mystique says, giggling, and even sillier, two girls alone on a Saturday night.

No sillier than two boys. Look at these two. At least women have something to say to each other. They don't get drunk out of their senses just to pass out.

I want a man. Oh boy. Mystique giggles again. Forgive me, hon, at my age.

Oh come off it. You want one of mine. Mario?

Please. Tell me, what's happening with horny Henry?

Too horny for his own good.

And the Pale Knight of the Night?

Julian? Fading away. He spends too much time on the West Side.

Mystique walks Lulu back home, waits on the stoop until the front door bangs shut and takes a cab back home, her legs unable to carry her. Lulu climbs her stairs wearily, visualizing her bed, the pillow in which she will sink, the fan turned on, blowing warm air on her sweaty nape. When she reaches the half-landing between the fourth and the fifth floor, she feels a presence, maybe somebody breathing.

She sees the leg first, the bottom of the jeans, will remember later the brown naked arms, the round shoulders coming out of the sleeveless T-shirt, the hands rolling a small piece of paper, the tight black curls hanging over the forehead. She stands on the last step, holding onto the railing, wondering if she should rush back down, if she has a chance, if he'd get up, pursue her. But he just gives her a level look, raising his eyes, not moving an inch.

Hi, he says. I'm Mario.

The man with
the white Pumas

He could be a junkie, a pusher, he looks like all those who wait at the street corners, who stomp their feet in the cold, in the humid, suffocating summer dust, who wait for the rallying cry to rush through the death maze and get their bag of dope, hands trembling, calming their sweats with candy bars. He's got eyes like black olives.

Come in, Lulu says, unlocking her door. She lets him walk in first. He isn't very tall, his T-shirt sparkling white. He goes straight to the couch, drops on it, a foot on the table, folding his knee over the elbow rest. He acts tough. He plays with a yellow plastic lighter he pulls out of his back pocket, with which he lights up a joint.

Do you want some?

Unh-unh.

He could be one of those who climb up the back of the buildings, dark as night, who hoist themselves from floor to floor, lift up the window left open on hot nights, with just the push of an elbow. These men are like cats who jump from roof to roof, swing on a rope from the cornice, leap through a top-floor window, invincible supermen. They brush away the glass they just pulverized, they have cats' eyes, they slide in the dark toward the tv set, the stereo, the family jewelry generally hidden in the same predictable place. They smell cash, cool cash, walk right to it, most of the time the victim is asleep, they don't need to twist their blade between thumb and forefinger, juggle it from hand to hand, in a combat pose, knee forward, balanced on their hips.

You're racist, she thinks. You're fucking racist! Just because he's got a dark skin and white Pumas. Just because he smells of the street, you see him as drug dealer, robber, rapist.

She watches him smoke. He's got thick, rough fingers.

So you are Mario, she says.

She'll remember that later.

So you are Mario. A confirmation of the image she's already formed in her mind.

Mario is sitting in front of her on the couch. He keeps pulling on his joint and his eyes take on an unnatural glaze.

Why did you keep calling me? she asks.

Oh, that's quite a story, he says, laughing. His laugh has a horselike quality, neighing almost, like sucking in the air in big gasps.

What's so funny?

You really want to know?

He tries to explain but it seems too complicated for words. Lulu listens politely. He asks, hey, you got some beer? He tells her they didn't mean to hassle her personally, but some people had been busted, and they thought Sarah had screwed them up. He's real sorry. What are you talking about? Lulu asks. He says he really can't talk about it, there're people involved in Loisaida and in Harlem, he says drugs is a cover for it. For what? she asks, Puerto Rican Liberation Front? He says he can't talk about it. He just wanted to know who she was, what she was up to. You've got some nerve, she says. She looks at his hands, he's rolling and unrolling an empty matchbook. He says, I didn't make the phone calls. My friend did. Oh, she says. And all the time I thought I recognized your voice. Cross my heart, he says. He crosses his heart. I swear it wasn't me. I believe you, she says, thinking, why the hell would I believe him? He asks, do you mind if I make a phone call? In New York City, he adds, not long distance, laughing for no reason one of his neighing laughs. Go ahead, she says. She watches his body switch to Spanish, his two hands flying around, as he insists, begs for something, thunders, soothes into the phone cradled in his neck.

I gotta go, he says, after hanging up. He pats his pockets back and front, checking for wallet, keys, who knows, dope.

See you around.

Yeah. See you around.

This photo of a woman half-hidden behind the flap of a tent makes her horny. The woman is naked, bent to the side, her breasts heavy with very wide aureolas. The print is grainy with deep shadows on her belly, her thighs. Her crotch is a triangle of shade. There is a roundness, a plumpness to her. Her half-turned face is sucked in the dark, with long, straight hair falling over one cheek. Naked women make Lulu horny like her own naked body makes her horny. What makes her horny in men is a smell, a presence, a movement, a fleeting expression in their eyes, their shoulders, their hands, life running through them and flickering in odd shapes and moods. Men usually don't seem to flaunt the sensuality of their bodies the way women do, reveling in their own curves and lines. The men she likes do it. Thrusting their asses out, abandoning their stretched armpits, their open legs, their erections to a woman's gaze.

She ran into Mario in the street and he asked her if she'd care to go to Manhattan Beach. It was the middle of the week and she said, why not, let me just get my bathing suit. They rode the train for an hour and when they got there it was crowded almost like a Sunday afternoon. There were bodies spread solid over more than a mile and criss-crossing rock 'n' roll and rap beats blaring from the boxes. In the brilliant blue sky a white banner flapped behind a biplane saying NOXZEMA COOLS THE BURN FAST. Vendors were walking up and down the beach loaded with brown paper bags chanting Hot knishes! Cold soda! Italian ice! Diet soda! There were pretty Puerto Rican girls so sexy with their clingy bathing suits in neon fuschia and turquoise that Lulu wondered why Mario had asked her to go with him. But he lay down next to her and played with soda-pop tops in the sand and looked at her with his olive eyes and she picked up a straw lying around and blew softly on his hands. Their bodies moved toward each other on his big beach towel with a Mickey Mouse on it and he stretched his legs along hers and they kissed. His tongue tasted of salt and grass and melted in her mouth.

Julian rang her bell in the middle of the night. She hadn't seen him in weeks. Instantly, before hearing his voice on the intercom, she knew who it was. He was so pale, his cheeks sucked in, his forehead oversized in comparison, sweat pearling on it. He wiped it off with a handkerchief. It scared her. She had never seen him strung out. His eyes were swimming in every direction. She didn't remember that his hands were so bony. What's the matter? she asked. He had big black combat boots and he stomped about the living room. What do you want? But of course she knew before he even opened his mouth. She couldn't believe that she'd ached for him so. She stared into his eyes and he turned them down to look for a cigarette. I'm sorry, she said, but I'm really broke right now. Shit! Just a ten or something. I'll give it back to you. There was a whiny edge to his voice. I can't, she said, I haven't paid the rent in two months. But she pulled out two fives from her wallet, grateful that he hadn't asked for more.

Mario makes her rice and beans in a big pot, big enough for a whole family, she says, laughing, stuffing herself, and he brings a dip of hot guacamole homemade with jalapeño peppers that burn her tongue but she keeps going at it late at night with a double bag of tortilla chips until the bowl is wiped clean, sunshine plate. Hot peppers make her giddy like liquor. He spends the night, tight and brown next to her, and brings her coffee in bed. He is dependable, in his way. Makes dates with her and keeps them. Wouldn't dream of not staying the night when he comes to her place. When she goes out with him another world opens up, a world she barely stares at like a stage when she walks around the neighborhood by herself. A world of *nuevos* and *nuevas, niños* and *niñas* and *abuelas* and *chiquitas* and *mamitas*. And *primos*. Everybody a *primo,* related to him in a convoluted way, marriage or blood, good or bad. Often bad. They sit around narrow apartments just like hers, except theirs are for real, with a handful of squeaking kids, popping half-Buds, listening to *salsa* blaring out of extra-large boxes sitting atop the kitchen table. Eating spicy roasts bursting with golden fat.

Te quiero, Mario tells her, and she grabs his thick black hair in her hands, losing her breath in his mouth.

Julian came back to her again one night and tried to put his soft cock into her but couldn't and she moved away from him horrified at her own disgust for this shriveling turnip slithering in the vicinity of her thighs, moist from piss or a drop of sperm that had wandered there accidentally. Not that she'd ever wanted him just hard and phallic, but his whole body was shrinking from the dope, he was burning a hole through himself from the core out. He still had bones, and flesh hanging to them, but inside was red-hot lava licking his organs. She thought the heart was already gone.

He cradled behind her back, pushed his knees up on his chest, wrapped his arms around his shoulders. All he wanted, he'd said, was warmth, human presence. He folded himself as a foetus but she refused to play mama. She kept her eyes wide open in the dark counting his heartbeats, thinking things were coming to a head, but she didn't know what.

Henry decides
to get married

Henry picks Lulu up at the Blue Night Lounge in a cab and starts dipping into her pants right away. I've got to tell you, he says, as the cab turns into dark narrow streets near the Hudson River. There's somebody staying at my place. A woman I met in the subway not that long ago. Beautiful, real young. Studying to be a graphic artist. I'm sure you'll like her. I want to marry her.

This time Lulu yanks his hand out.

You mean to say you've just decided to get married and the girl is staying with you and you're still taking me to your place?

Sure, he says, taking her hand to his lips and running his tongue between the fingers. Lulu pulls her hand away. She knows about you. I tell you: I know you two are going to like each other. Oh, here we are. Thanks, Henry says to the cabdriver, cramming three singles into the plastic tray toward the front part of the cab. Keep the change.

They get out. Henry makes a motion with his arm behind Lulu's back to invite her to step into his building. Lulu stands in the middle of the sidewalk without moving.

What are we going to do? Sit around the coffee table and watch the boats on the river? Or leaf through your new lithos and exclaim what a talented artist you are? Or fuck all together?

Now. Now. Lulu. Whatever we feel like. Sherry knows about other women in my life. She wouldn't dream of trying to stop any of my relationships. Besides, she has her own room.

Is she going to bring us breakfast in bed?

We might all have breakfast together. Come on, let's go.

I am not going up, Lulu says.

Why not? It's not the first time you've seen my other lovers. Come on.

It's the first time you tell me you're going to get married.

I'm sorry, Lulu. I didn't mean to hurt your feelings. You know I love you. Come.

But they walk down the street then all the way to the piers. The river is thick, it smells of oil and faintly of putrefaction, as if it carried corpses to the ocean. Henry is pressing her to his side, his naked arm brushing against her cheeks. The night is warm. The summer never seems to end. The night heat has the sweetness of death. Battery Park City farther south looks like the specter of a future city of the dead rising out of the vacant lots, and they stop to look at it, Henry stroking his beard pensively, having run out of words, or explanations, or interest.

You, getting married, Lulu says. You must be kidding!

I was married once, you know.

But what about your freedom, all your lovers . . .

There is something special between us. She's like pure diamond. She's strong, earthy. She's wild like quickfire. She makes me want to have children with her. She's my woman.

Did you tell her that already?

She feels the same about me.

You're getting old, Henry.

Maybe. Maybe the time has come.

Slowly they head back toward Henry's loft. His lips are moist and greedy, his hands feeling their way into her clothes.

Sherry is only here for a week, he says. I'll call you after she leaves.

A storm

I am a hole. I am completely hollow inside with limbs quivering at the periphery of myself. Each man who makes me wet shoots a hole through my guts and then I leak words of love and all my insides spill out. Us girls are hollowed out when we grow up so that we always crave for a man. We writhe about, searching for strong hands to knead our flesh, every one of our apertures dying to be filled with their fingers, cocks, tongues swelling, swirling, to be turned into lava, dripping juices. Then the next morning they're gone and we're a big gaping wound. We grab a pillow, we suck on a chocolate bar. And we never hear of them again. Or they call back ten days later, matter-of-fact, asking, did I leave my sweater at your place by any chance? Oh great. Do you mind dropping it off for me at the café across the street? Thanks a bunch. No. I don't think I'll have the time to see you. I'm going on vacation to Europe tomorrow. *Ciao*, baby.

The orange cat stretches out on the windowsill in Lulu's kitchen. The night is hot, abnormally hot, even for the end of summer in New York City. All of Lulu's fans are buzzing, rotating slowly and diligently. The drought is getting severe because the winter has been too warm, especially in the Midwest, plagued by successive heat waves, with light or nonexistent precipitation, and the temperatures are still a good ten degrees warmer than normal. This seems like a confirmation of the theory that the world is getting hotter due to the diffusion of gases in the upper atmosphere. In the streets people are fanning themselves with newspapers, invitation cards to parties or clubs, and drop by at air-conditioned restaurants for a breath of cool air. It's hot like at midday, but in the dark the heat is ominous, just like during a total eclipse of the sun the darkness is ominous and in fact dangerous, since you can't go out without sunglasses to protect your eyes from getting burned.

Lulu goes to sleep like she almost always does when she is alone, with the tv on, its soft synthetic hues and low-frequency murmur soothing her into a mesmerized trance.

At the corner of B and Sixth, Tillie the bag lady has discarded her blankets and jacket and thrown them on the couch. She's kept her hat on, though, she would never be caught in the street without it, she struts around the couch in small bouncing steps, her flesh quivering around her upper arms, a painful grin on her face because her swollen ankles hurt each time her feet hit the ground. She opens her arms and sings with a surprising low-pitched voice, swirling around and around until she collapses on the couch, laughing uncontrollably. The heat is getting suffocating and the first rumbles of an electrical storm pound in the night.

Lulu dreams of rockets smashing through the sky. She is caught among a crowd of people when the nuclear alarms go off. Nobody's heard a nuclear alarm before and nobody knows what it sounds like, and maybe there is no such thing as a nuclear alarm, but somehow the alarms are so alarming that there cannot be any doubt. This is Fifth Avenue at Rockefeller Center on a hot Saturday afternoon and the crowds freeze. Simultaneously the rockets smash through the sky, etc. One after the other the skyscrapers go up in flames. People seek refuge in the shops, swoop down the sunken area used as a skating rink in the wintertime, throw themselves on the ground, bodies covering bodies, some dying right here, smothered under each other's weight.

Half-awake, Lulu hugs her bed with her outstretched arms, realizing a smoke alarm's gone off in somebody's apartment, shrieking through the floors, and the building's being hit by lightning: flashes of light pour through the night crashing down like rockets again and again. It's a giant fist pounding down the roof down the street. So this is why the ancients believed in the Thunder God. The sky is black purple with ghosts of white glimmer flashing through, vanishing above the rooftops toward the east.

Once I dreamed my mother tried to make love to me. She had the white plump body of her photographs but no face. I dreamed she was in bed with me and she cradled me in her arms like a baby. But then her hand lifted my nightgown, oh so gently, it brushed the inside of my thighs as if by accident, her fingers ran up my chest and she pressed her body against mine, her naked leg entwined with mine. I received the full weight of her body, her heavy breasts in my neck. I woke up, my hands in my crotch pressing hard trying to chase the dream away.

It is 3 A.M. Pouring rain like a tidal wave crashing against the windows. Lulu's apartment pitches heavily in the roaring storm. Manhattan is a ship-island tossed about the swollen seas swept by the winds. All the lights are off, except the lightning is discharging at an incredible speed, zipping down the electric lines, through her belly, through her entrails bleeding softly, the fullness of her ovaries, the uterus tightening like a fist. Sitting cross-legged in the middle of the mattress she clutches her body, the tide of the storm rising and exploding, rising and exploding.

I wake up, startled, gasping for breath. I sit on the side of the bed, my legs hanging in the long nightshirt. The lace collar is too tight around my neck. It's dawn and a three-forked hatrack stands out against the white curtain. My chest is tight, my breath comes out whistling through my throat in short, panicky bursts. I struggle to open the button. Then I try to sleep again. If only I could sleep.

My aunt moves in the dim light, her massive body trapped into a tight black dress as she swiftly walks to my bed. She's up so early. Doing what? There's no cow to milk, here, no hen cackling in the backyard looking for seeds. Her hands, breaking loose out of the long sleeves, are dry on my forehead. This kid's sick, she says. Aren't you cold? She tightens my collar. I can't breathe. I try to push the hands away. Let me do it, *ma chérie*. You'll feel better.

(Your aunt again, Salvine will say when Lulu reads the passage aloud to her later. Why is it always women who do it to women?)

The hands fly over my body. I close my eyes, let my head drop on the thick pillow she slides under me.

Accept the short breath. Don't fight it. Breathe only at ten percent of your lungs' capacity. Don't move, don't waste energy. Live under the hand which weighs on your chest, swim underneath, in the muddy waters of drowsiness.

She comes back with the syrup. It flows thick and sweet in my throat. Sometimes when I stay up at night, when I toss about in my bed without finding sleep, when I count the sheep grazing in an apple-green pasture, or when I close my eyes tight and concentric circles glide at a dizzying speed under my eyelids in electric pink, scarlet, vermilion, steel blue, onyx black, adamantine flashes, I go get the syrup in the cabinet over the bathroom sink and drink from it in big gulps, then I crouch on the bed, the covers pulled up over my head.

The syrup doesn't put me to sleep right away. The bed swings. *Jouir est coupable,* pleasure is sinful, she yells from the jetty, stiff in her twenty-year-old body I remember from the photos, while I run away on the shore, barefoot, hitching my skirt on my sandy calves, looking for this other, unreachable world. But I can't see it, I am caged in a room with one-way mirrors, I bang against them with my fists. I roam the room looking for the other side, did she ever suspect its existence?

My body coated with oil, I slip along the light beam under my bedroom door, then arching my thighs around the banister I slide down the stairs and thread my way between the shutter slots. Escaping her vigilance.

The sand runs hot between my fingers as I gather it in small handfuls. It crackles and burns my skin.

. . . *Coupable!* she yells again like an echo, but I can barely hear her voice in the wind as I run.

The storm has washed the sky clean. Limpid baby-blue. Pure ozone lifting the heart. Bluejays peeping loud in the cherry trees. The rap beat on the boxes rising sharp and clear in the light morning air. Pungent smell of the earth drenched deep, opening its pores to the sun already darting hot. The New York Mutual Insurance Building flashing its brass top like a monogrammed gold tooth.

Lulu goes dancing down the street. She's got a flaming red mane bouncing about her shoulders and wings at her heels. Her heart flies, she glides a couple of yards above the sidewalk, she even welcomes the dogshit rising in powerful smells from the dog run in the park. Puppies are jumping around on the grassless mound. They caracole at the end of their leashes, swinging on their hindlegs. *L'amour est enfant de Bohême, tala-tata-tala-tata-tata. Il me dit des mots d'amour, des mots de tous les jours. Je t'aime.* He's got bronze skin, Indian blood running through his veins, and black blood from the African slaves imported to the West Indies, mixed with Spanish *sangre de conquistadores*. He's got the master and the slave within him and he comes from the center of the Americas, the point where the South and the North, the First and the Third World, the right and the left clash over a string of paradise islands. This is ridiculous. What is he, a small-time drug dealer, high school dropout, freelance construction worker and house painter, part-time bartender, full-time lover and wheeler-dealer. Or what? She still feels his hands all over her body, he left his mark on her. He says he believes in voodoo and wears a gris-gris around his neck.

There is a Peeping Tom who watches me get undressed from the backyard. He leaves small messages scribbled in a childlike hand that he rolls and pushes under my bedroom window. They're full of clichés about my alabaster breasts and my ass like a gleaming moon. I spy on him through the shutters. I've discovered someone has brought a cinderblock under my window. An adult could stand on it and his eyes would be at the right level. I leave the light on at night and slowly peel my baby-doll off my shoulders, my hips, my thighs, and masturbate in front of the window with my legs wide open. The messages become more and more explicit and I think things are getting out of hand, so I tell my aunt about someone spying in the garden and she launches a man hunt while I keep undressing with the light on.

Mario tells her *te quiero* and she thinks Spanish is a language that believes in passion. Not I love you but I want you. Less romantic maybe but *te quiero* is about eroticism, and *te quiero* is what he means. She doesn't know if he loves her. She doesn't know if she loves him. She doesn't know what love is. *Te quiero también, Mario.* He's got fire running in his veins. She can smell it on his breath.

Noon Dragon

Lulu goes down for *cuchifritos* at the stand near the corner *bodega*. There she doesn't have to worry whether she is French or American, it's all in Spanish without subtitles. The owner at first raised an eyebrow in surprise that her Spanish had no trace of Anglo-Saxon drawl. Now he pours down her ear a stream of PR-accented *castillano* she has trouble hanging onto. She orders the chicken wings wrapped in a blanket of fried batter thick and white inside like dumplings. Then she pictures the grease lining up the inside of her arteries after each mouthful, yellow cushions of fat, and her blood fighting its way along tighter and tighter pipes. Of course this may be a fiction. But to be on the safe side she usually subsists on a diet of fruit and raw vegetables, because in this city anything at the wrong end of the sugar line or the grease or chemical line is considered evil, punished by fatal diseases. She doesn't want to be consumed in hell's fatty flames. Why die when you can live forever? But secretly she longs for evil *soupes de poissons* laced with mercury, or creamy veal chops bathed in hormone sauce like they do in Paris, it makes her salivate. Then she jogs fifteen times around the park in punishment for wanting to be so sinful.

American corpses have so many chemicals stored in them nowadays, announces the tv reporter, that they've stopped disintegrating in their graves. Whereas there used to be a reasonably quick turnover of corpses in the common graves, leaving sufficient room on top for fresh ones, contemporary corpses threaten to be preserved eternally, which is creating a serious problem of overpopulation in our cemeteries.

At home the little girl is always washing her hands. She eats. She washes her hands. She shits, she washes her hands. She reads a book, she washes her hands. She holds a pen for five minutes, she washes her hands. She helps herself from a glass of apple juice, she washes her hands. She looks at herself in the mirror she washes her hands. She touches herself she washes her hands. She touches herself down there. Again and again. It smells on her fingers. She washes her hands. Several times in a row. She wipes herself with the towel. She washes her hands. She washes her hands she washes her hands. The water runs on her hands, she holds the soap she washes her hands. She touches the tap she washes her hands. She washes her hands she washes her hands. She washes her hands she washes her hands she washes her hands she washes her hands she washes her hands

It's paranoid psychosis, says the psychiatrist.

I was four or five. First day in school. We had to wear beige bloomers at gym class. Us girls. The boys wore beige shorts. There were about fifteen little boys around cavorting and carrying on. As many little girls, already tamed, trained to wait around. I looked at my thighs, round, white. I thought the other kids were staring at them, but I was the one who stared, my back against the courtyard wall. I think I remember (or do I make this up?) the chestnut trees, the big, pawlike leaves casting deep shadows in the October afternoon, the chill on my naked legs and feeling so exposed, anonymous. We were arranged in a square formation, jumping up and down in rows of five, breathe in and out, don't forget to breathe, the gym teacher was yelling, a whistle hanging by a chain between her flat breasts, I want to see your arms in a nice *V* above your shoulders, a *V*, I said, Chantal, don't you know your alphabet yet? Then flap the side of your thighs with your hands as you go down. Up and down, up and down.

Salvine turns off the tape recorder.

That's not the kind of thing you want, right? Lulu asks.

I don't know. Maybe it is. It's part of it. It's like a puzzle. Sometimes you can only get it when all the pieces have been fitted together.

And how will you know that all the pieces are there?

Maybe we'll never get all the pieces.

Lulu looks at her sideways. Maybe one day I'll stop feeding you the pieces.

Salvine gets up.

Let me make us some tea, she says. Talking about puzzles. I want to show you this antique one I bought. All made of wood. There're some fragments missing, but I think it makes it more intriguing.

In the rundown playground, kids play in the dust. A tiny little boy waves a wooden sword, or rather a slat of pinewood, its point sharpened like an arrow with the words NOON DRAGON spray-painted in red on it. He points it at an older girl armed with an umbrella. They cross weapons. Noon Dragon against blue umbrella. Whoosh, whoosh. The girl roars, goes for the kill. Her umbrella is longer. She could impale him. Noon Dragon takes fright. He flees, his sword jolting behind him. The girl runs after him, *ven aqui, ven aqui* she yells, but he's gone, swallowed by a dark opening cut into a wall of cinderblocks.

BOY 3, KILLS BABY BROTHER

A three-year-old Manhattan boy shot his baby brother dead yesterday. The child found a loaded .38 Colt handgun under a pillow in his parents' bedroom. Thinking it was a toy, the child took the gun to his room, cocked it, pulled the trigger and shot his eighteenth-month-old brother in the head. The baby died in the hospital. The father had bought the gun "for protection" after his house had been burglarized two years ago.

Everybody Lulu knows in New York lives in transient apartments. Two, three, four rooms without a hallway, lofts with the paint peeling off the walls, shelves of books and a few useless objects scavenged from previous lives in other apartments or lofts on the other side of the country, on the other side of the Atlantic, shared with former lovers or groups of friends, alienated from parents, siblings, their own culture, their country, the rest of the world, hanging onto Manhattan by their fingernails for fear of falling back into America's wasteland.

Lulu's apartment is all vinyl and pink marbleized Formica. Lavender and pink neons pulsating on the ceilings and the walls. The apartment is only a sublet, but she couldn't stand the old dusty woodfloor, so she decided to paint it a glossy lime green. Too bad if Sarah didn't like it. In New York you create your own reality. You make yourself a set and costumes and you launch your life. If it doesn't work, you start all over with a different plot, a different set of characters. It's totally artificial. A man-made product. Sometimes beautiful. But unreal. It doesn't take certain things into account: like being born, death, aging, the process of living. It's a crazed merry-go-round, with bodies flying off the side when they can't hold onto the horses anymore. Now who's sweeping up the corpses? Somebody's got to do the dirty job.

Lulu cuts the news items, puts them away (the clippings now fill
two fat folders), and lights up two candles, one red, one green.
One for love (passion variety), one for money. She watches the
melted wax lick its way to the saucers, wishing hard.

What do you wish for, Lulu? Nothing. Everything. It's a kind
of prayer. The two candles, the red and the green, keep guard,
their flames casting long shadows on the greasy kitchen wall,
warming up Lulu's wishes into magical fluids. Lulu, who stopped
going to Mass after her Confirmation but can still taste the flat
unleavened taste of the Holy Host on her palate. Small discreet
altar, with the candles burning to Fate, the faceless God.

After the funny war my family moved to the South. They had a
house there, an old farmhouse with pink-washed walls, its back
to the railroad tracks. It had a big garden full of shadows and
bushes. The gate opened on a pebbled alley that led straight to
a garage covered with honeysuckle and wild roses tumbling over
the door. Inside the house the walls were lined with *toile de Jouy*,
traditional sea or country scenes on canvas, in faded pinks and
blues. The atmosphere was genteel. A bourgeois house in a small
village. Except they had Jews hidden in the toolshed at the back
of the garden. But that was later. First they fled Paris, occupied
by the Germans. The bomber planes going down like thunder,
the explosions like lightning, blue and yellow crashes shattering
the windows, *à plat ventre*, belly down, arms crossed behind
head in protection, run run to the shelters, hundreds of them
panting hugging each other, children screaming. I was not one
of these children. I was born in the dead, shell-shocked fifties.
My cousin was a child of the war, raised in the *maquis* near
Grenoble, the family legend goes it was so cold in the unheated
hut, stalactites were running from his nose on winter nights, and
he almost froze to death in the backwoods at the foot of the
Alps.

In the South they didn't have to wait in line with their food tickets for a few ounces of margarine and some rutabaga, a double ration of milk if there was a pregnant woman in the family. They had eggs and milk and butter and poultry and fresh vegetables. They went back to the old lifestyle they knew so well. In a weird way they were happier. They didn't have to think about climbing the social ladder. They could sit around the fireplace at night with the farmers and the schoolteachers and the town hall clerks and chat about the harvests and the war news as if it was from another country. But when my mother fell in love with a Jew, they had to take sides and there was the question of loyalties and anti-Semitism and social conventions and life and death and the war penetrated them like a knife through the heart. They would never be the same again.

The last passions died with the liberation. I was raised with the tales of sublime and shrewd resistance and heroic daily survival but my reality was post-war pettiness and hysteria in a vain attempt to revive pre-war order.

Hanging on to photos is like trying to control time, or your life, Lulu says to Mystique, who frantically searches for snapshots of her and her friends in the sixties.

But it was a time, it was a time . . . Even that is gone, then what is left? We might as well die at the next breath.

You've got your memory.

But memory distorts.

So do photos. You try to arrange your past in neat little boxes of photos, letters, documents, cards, ribbons, odds and ends and you think you can open a box and here pops out that day or that season or that period. Here pops out the old you. But it doesn't. That old you is more alive in you now than in any box of memorabilia. What's the past anyway? It's a mood, a color, a quality of fear, rage, passion, despair, and what you're looking for is to strike the same note again. You don't really care if you had less wrinkles then or if your hair looked different. What you want is to recall what it felt like to be alive in 1957, 1965, 1972. As if life were more intense then, when you were younger, the wine tasted better, the sun was hotter, the ocean more breath-taking, rock 'n' roll more powerful, love more devastating . . .

I found them, Mystique says. Are you finished with your speech? I'll show you what a tart I looked.

This? This is you? But this is not the sixties?

For me it was. Early sixties.

Push-up bra, girdle, teased hair in a beehive, beige foundation, mauve lipstick. Lulu laughs. Did you really look like that? I bet it must be weird for you to see it all come back.

I'm glad I found them, Mystique says. They reassure me that I wasn't a figment of my imagination.

But you were a product of your imagination. And you still are right now, Lulu says, turning the tv on to MTV with the sound down. Let's go through your clothes. Let's get dressed tonight. Come on, let's make ourselves into sixties bad girls.

Mystique powders her nose. She uses very white compact powder, Japanese, that she applies with a flat painter's brush, until she looks completely livid. She likes that makeup. It's a mask under which she can come and go as she damn well pleases. She sinks her eyes into two pools of grey and charcoal shades and slashes her face with a purple mouth.

Lulu borrows a dress from her, cinched at the waist, and makes herself doe eyes.

Don't forget the *mouche,* Mystique says, before they walk out into the sultry night.

That same night the kid was doing graffiti in the subway. He was spraying his black angry tag, RAID, in skinny tortuous letters on every door of the train. That night was special. He was going to write up something he'd been thinking about for a while. His plan was to use the whole length of the train. He had a stock of brand new vermilion-red spray cans, he was deep in the yards, in front of a greyish car, just done over by the MTA cleaning squad with their new paint, the kind that supposedly is graffiti-repellent, can be washed off with a sponge and water. But he didn't give a fuck about that. He picked up the can and moved his hand way high, steadied it and pressed the valve. The hand went straight down like for an *L* or an *I*, and then they were on him. He couldn't tell how many they were. They were swift and professional. He didn't scream, he tried to spray in their eyes, but they caught his move and pushed his arm away. The spray went off on the subway car, a splash of red dripping like blood down to the wheel, and the can flew out of his hand. In a matter of seconds he was strapped in a strait jacket of arms and legs wrapped around his neck, groin and torso. He kicked his heels and tried to fling his elbows around, but they had him in a steel grip. Worse: vicious. That's when he realized they were cops. But they didn't handcuff him. They kicked him around for a while, then went down to serious business. It was 4 A.M. and the yard was dark like thick brew. When he stopped fighting back they called an ambulance and took him to the hospital, where he was pronounced DOA.

The papers said he died of a heart attack while resisting arrest.

The atomic
mushroom

Mario is the son of a drug dealer from Avenue C and Twelfth Street. He says his old man only deals coke and grass, some pills, but no heroin. His family lives in a three-room apartment over a *botánica,* where his mother purchases her regular supplies of candles and scents for her *santería* sessions. He started taking drugs when he was twelve, but he's cleaned up his act now. He saw too many kids his age go off the deep end. Junkies at fourteen, in the joint at eighteen, OD'ed at twenty-one. My best friend when I was growing up is in the joint for murder, he says, he's got thirty years. Man, I don't want to fuck up my life like that. Sure I was shooting up. Look: see my arms? No tracks. Smooth as baby's skin. I haven't taken any junk for four years, and I want to stay clean. My father, he is no bad man. He is just supporting his family. Drug dealing is the only job around here. Man, you've got to understand. My father's family, they were peasants. They were fucking starving in Puerto Rico.

Mario reads the *Daily News* report about the kid's death in the subway, allegedly of a heart attack.

A heart attack, gimme a break. The guy was what, twenty-four, twenty-five? It must've been a hell of a scare to give him a heart attack. The pigs! It's open season in this city on the blacks and the spics.

Maybe he had too much cholesterol, Lulu says.

Say what?

Never mind.

Mario still lives in the neighborhood. He's got a room at the back of an after-hours bar. He likes to feel the crowd pulsing, the smell of spilled beer, of sweat, it helps him fall asleep. He says it's like being in a big, warm, noisy womb. He never finished high school, but he calls himself an autodidact—a word he learned from a jazz musician who used to hang out at the bar. The guy told him that people who never went to school are autodidacts because they've had to learn everything by themselves. That's me, Mario said. Now he tends the bar from time to time, deals some dope and tries to get his shit together.

It really is a mushroom, a flamboyant fuschia mushroom eerily rising up in a purple sky. The lines are so pure, the aureola-like crown of smoke curling above the long, slender stem so other-wordly, it takes your breath away. On another picture it looks like a gigantic cotton ball fluffed on the aquamarine horizon, at the edge of a surrealistic landscape reflected on a reddish sea, a serene inhabited mineral world. Or it froths on a deep cobalt background, bursting from a sea of clouds that seem to be shredding into entangled yarns of blue wool. One resembles a huge upside-down glass of glistening red crystal hanging from a huge upside-down red plate, floating against a backdrop of wine-colored velvet. When Lulu came across these photos of the atomic mushroom in an old art magazine at the Jefferson Market Library, she pretended to take the magazine back to the shelves and, making sure nobody was paying attention, ripped the pages off the binding. The shots were taken during test explosions of the A-bomb somewhere in the Pacific Ocean in the forties and fifties. They are visions of post-apocalyptic grandeur evoking the dawn of time, perhaps ours, perhaps a future prehistoric universe waiting to be peopled. This is death radiating in the seductive hues of Cinemascopic brilliance. It has the beauty of a natural calamity, of a tidal wave, of a volcano erupting, of glaciers spreading down toward the tropics in minutes instead of millennia. The ambiguity of so much beauty in total destruction is disturbing like a secret death-wish. Was our world born of an atomic explosion, Lulu wonders, as, back at her apartment, she clips the glossy photos, carefully cutting their edges with a razor blade, and tacks them on the wall over her bed. How many lived-in planets has the history of the universe known? How many cycles of birth, civilization, and explosion? Why does the Bible talk about Armageddon? Did the prophets know, from past lives, from intuition, from knowledge deeply imbedded in human minds, that worlds are cyclical, that humanity will have an end, and maybe blew itself up in the past? But then in the Dark Ages they all thought the world would come to an end in the year 1000 and nothing happened. Maybe it's got something to do with the power of numbers, and now the year 2000 approaching while the nuclear sword swings over our heads . . .

Mario's laugh is infectious. It carries the intensity of his tight, compact body, it snaps and spills out in short bursts, releasing his trapped energy like a froth from his lips, jumpy waves quivering on the surface of his body. He is an electrified high wire. He laughs and her skin prickles. I like your laugh, Lulu says, it makes me think of sex, I forbid you to laugh with other women. Desire is between the legs of the beholder, he replies. When I was little, they used to say I laughed like a donkey. You know, hee-ha, hee-ha. Hardly a sex symbol. Mario asks Lulu how she says fuck in French. *Baiser,* she says, which also means *beso,* a kiss. But I prefer to say *faire l'amour,* it's sexier than *to make love.* Yes, he repeats, *faire l'amour.* He has a dazzling smile, all teeth, a big, generous mouth with purple lips that flow like silk along her body, up and down curves and hills, when he laughs tiny lines form on his smooth brown skin, stretching his eyes to almonds. You never know, until he laughs, which will appear, the velvet tenderness in his eyes, or the razorblade, sharp, don't-fuck-wit'-me gleam switching out and in so fast you're not sure you actually saw it, it just cuts through your guts leaving you breathless. But then he bursts into laughter and you laugh with him, you can't resist, you want to eat his laugh up, eat his soul through his lips, suck the marrow out of him, this energy he has, you want to feel it run through your veins, his *sangre de Africanos*. You've got madness in your eyes, madness in your laugh, Lulu says. I love men who have madness in them. Who are still a little bit uncontrollable. Watch out what you saying, he says. He's biting her lips. His two canines stick out a little, they're a bit twisted and end up in sharp triangles. Vampire! Don't laugh, he warns her, pushing her with his whole body on the couch, his sex hard bulging under his 501 button-down fly, rolling with her from the couch to the carpet, down onto the lime-green lacquered floor all the way to the wall, stop it, she says, stop it! You're choking me! I thought you liked uncontrollable men, he says.

Prenez du coquelicot, mesdames, prenez du coquelicot!

Tillie is only a part-time bag lady. She's got an apartment on the first floor of a run-down tenement with broken windows and a lockless front door yawning in the wind, all the tenants in that building are squatters, except her. She was a legitimate rentee when the landlord decided to cut the electricity and stop filling up the boiler and collecting the rent, but she stayed on, watching the others pack up and move out, because she'd been there for twenty years and had no other place to go. She was also attached to the stray cats she fed on the stoop every day. Someone gave her a little portable gas heater and that was enough for the wintertime until the real cold hit. When it froze too hard she went to the Salvation Army for the night and for hot meals and she fell into the habit of going there even in good weather to save on food stamps, and then one year she got cut off from Welfare without knowing why and she didn't bother to find out, she just drifted toward the shelters and in the summertime spent a lot of time in the street, sitting on an abandoned couch or a stoop warmed up by the sun until she dozed off. But a last thread of memory brought her periodically back to her apartment and the cats. She picked up metal scraps and old fabrics and beer cans out of the garbage and in the park alleys, and with the money she made from that bought food for the cats and if there was some left over, for herself, then she went home and spent days leafing through old newspapers and rummaging around, shuffling piles of plastic bags full of old clothes and scrapped kitchen utensils or just sitting at the front window slightly below street level watching legs and feet go by as if she was at the seashore.

Prenez du coquelicot, mesdames, prenez du coquelicot!

Lulu wears blue, cerulean blue, brilliant. *Bleu des mers du Sud.* A blue sweatshirt she peels off before the show, blue cotton pants that drop to her ankles when she pops the snap. Her naked legs are shivering in the cold. The dressing room is so drafty without a radiator. She folds her arms on her breasts, looking for the sequined top and G-string she wears for the go-go number. *Prenez du coquelicot, mesdames* . . . The thread is so tenuous. So . . . And if it breaks, then what's left? But of course there are other threads. A whole entangled cocoon. Everything is there in her memory, if only she had access to it. It's fucking cold in here, says Mystique, charging into the dressing room. I can't believe this place. We had an electric heater last winter, they took it away again! Ed walks in to beg for a cigarette, he knows Mystique always keeps a pack on the makeup table.

Mind if I take one? he says.

D'you know what happened to the radiator? Mystique asks.

He's so fucking stingy, Ed says, pointing with his thumb toward the entrance of the backroom where Marty, the manager,

officiates in a stiff black suit and starched white shirt. He probably figured he'd save on Con Ed bills. You guys look blue. Hey
listen, how about a shot of rum while you get ready? Hang on
here, be right back.

What a sweetheart, Mystique says.

We were walking on the beach at La Baule, Corinne and I.
Corinne was a friend of my aunt, a painter, whom I had known
since I was a child. She had short steel-grey hair cut like that of
a man. She was all steel and vigorous energy. The weather that
day was like her, grey, steely clouds drifting in the huge sky, its
boundaries lost in a smoky mist, a sea of lead receding, leaving
behind silver puddles and grey wet sand. It was fall, our rubber
boots made splash sounds as we walked at the edge of the water.
The seagulls glided low, letting themselves be pushed by the wind,
following the tide. There's something unique about the beach
off-season. It's as if nature regressed to a primitive stage, to a
state of solemn and indifferent power. We must've been talking
philosophy or about my future because that's what we talked
about when we were together. Corinne said she wanted to give
me a present. She pulled something out of her K-way raincoat
pocket, wrapped in a white handkerchief. It was a piece of some
transparent mineral. I asked her what it was, rolling it in my
hand. She said it was a crystal, and I felt its points and edges
with my fingers. Its transparency reflected the greyness around
us with a milky light. She told me it was an octahedron, did I
notice it's like two pyramids back to back? She said crystal
amplifies the higher consciousness, that I should keep it with me,
it would help me see the light when I was confused. I should
wash it once in a while in seawater—she cupped a little in her
hands and rubbed the crystal with it to show me—to recharge
its energy. I kept the crystal tight in my hand deep inside my
pocket. It fitted right inside my palm. As we walked it became
warm, the same warmth as my body.

Mario doesn't know about Henry, or Julian. Julian hasn't been
around lately, for one thing, and Henry . . . well, Henry is on

another plane, so to speak. Henry is like Salvine, they belong to another life, another dimension. Some could say that Lulu divides her life into boxes, countries, social circles, people, her mind, her sex, her memory. But Lulu doesn't divide really. She just happens to exist in different modes quasi-simultaneously. As far back as she can remember she has perceived herself in fragments at sharp angles with one another, like the facets on the crystal Corinne gave her years ago. Besides, she knows Mario couldn't deal with it. Ever met a Latin who's not jealous? he tells her. *Chica,* don't be naive. And what does a jealous Latin do, Mario? Don't mess with him, if you want my advice. But Henry takes her out to dinner in posh candlelit restaurants and she dresses up with high heels, hats and long satin gloves and *rouge baiser* lipstick that leaves a cherry mark on the linen napkin and on the edge of the crystal glass. She smokes his cigarettes in a tortoiseshell cigarette holder and he rolls up her skirts and takes her late at night on the king-size bed overlooking the Hudson, before the huge gilded mirror which reflects their half-dressed bodies twisted in suggestive poses. Julian knows about Henry. He calls him her saccharine daddy because she once told him Henry was trying to lose weight.

The child
eats her soup

Eat your soup, my aunt said. Her hips, encased in a blue-and-white gingham apron, leaned against the table, next to her dry hands which rested flat on the tablecloth, a foot away from my plate.

I said I was not hungry anymore, pushed my plate and set my spoon next to it. Her hands had long tapered fingers with fingernails filed oval and perfectly manicured with a clear polish. Raised purple veins formed a complicated pattern, intertwined with the very apparent fanlike bone structure. I hated these hands. One index finger moved abruptly toward me and touched the edge of the soup bowl. It's a good leek-and-potato soup. You have to finish your plate. It will make you grow tall and strong.

I shook my head.

Her hands grew threatening. You will have nothing else to eat until you finish your soup.

I folded my arms on my chest and kept my head down.

One hand came crashing down in front of me, shaking the table so that the soup made waves in the bowl, licking its edge, and a drop fell on the flat plate underneath. You little . . . I jumped.

The voice thinned to a thread whistled between the teeth.

Are you going to eat your soup, yes or no?

Slowly I picked up my spoon and began to move it around the thick liquid.

It's too hot, I said finally.

Blow on it.

She walked around the table and grabbed the spoon from me, blowing on it herself. Her thin lips gathered to an *O*, with a number of very fine lines converging on it. Open up! she hissed. I closed my mouth tight. The spoon hit my front teeth, spilling the soup on the tablecloth and my bib. The back of her hand slammed hard and dry on my cheek.

Open your mouth, I said!

I burst into tears, protecting my face with my folded arm.

Open your mouth, or I'll . . . Squeezing my wrist, leaving four red marks on my wrist.

I opened up and let the liquid go down my throat, four, five, six times, ten times, until the plate was wiped clean.

Did you hate France when you were growing up? asks Salvine.

I don't know. I didn't know what France was. I mean, I couldn't tell about the Frenchness of my growing up. I hated them.

Who are "them"?

I told you. Her. My father's family.

Your father?

No. Not my father. But listen. I don't want to talk about this anymore. You're not my shrink.

What about that scene you wrote? Did it have anything to do with your coming here?

No. Why would it? Not directly, at least. I didn't like her. I could've just moved out. I didn't have to leave my country for that. What made *you* come here?

Salvine looks out the window, at the grey sky heavy with rain. For the first time Lulu notices the skin going soft under her chin. Salvine's fingers hug the velvet of the bedspread, her nails dig into it. She keeps her eyes on the line of reddish-brown trees in the park. I wanted to know the world, she says. For me New York was the world. It was the center. It was Rome, it was Alexandria. It was Babylon! It was the stuff of my dreams . . .

Were you unhappy in Poitiers?

No. Not at all. In fact I was very much in love with this man you saw in the photo when I decided to leave. But I couldn't breathe. I didn't belong there. I came with a suitcase and a hundred dollars in my purse and I got a waitress job at a French restaurant in the west Forties. I lived in a rooming house with other French waitresses, right in the middle of Hell's Kitchen. We were two or three in a room. I was dirt poor, but I loved every minute of it. It was Life. It was Adventure. I'd go down to the piers and watch the French liners steam up the Hudson and dock, their hulls curving high above the piers, almost as high as skyscrapers, and I'd watch people pour off the gangplanks. To me they were like pilgrims flocking to pay their tribute to Mecca. New York was very different then. The fifties and early sixties were stuffy and uptight and politically paranoid. But when my ship entered New York bay and I first saw those glittering buildings rise literally out of the water, I knew it was the key to my spiritual journey.

Spiritual? It's pretty materialistic though.

New York has always been about a spiritual quest for me. I think the spirit of New York transcends its materialism. But we're supposed to talk about you.

Lulu shrugs. She's lying down on her stomach on the thick carpet, her silver-threaded basketball sneakers shimmering as she swings her ankles.

All right, she says, sitting up and crossing her legs. I ran away from her. I kept running away from her. But I always came back.

And then one time it was for good. I met an American man, real sweet, who paid for my plane ticket and got me a job as a receptionist in a big newspaper. I never went back.

But why New York?

Is there anywhere else?

Yes. Pittsburgh, Des Moines, Minneapolis . . .

Listen. I lived in Amsterdam for six months. I loved the little houses along the canals. It was so cute, so tame. So pretty. Like a doll's town. I thought I would die. Here I don't want to die. You know the story about the fly in the vat of milk? It was drowning and it got so freaked out it started to move its little legs around, you know, swimming, kind of, it kept moving them and moving them and moving them and it was getting harder and harder, but it kept going until it found itself sitting on top of a bowl of butter?

So?

That's how I feel in New York. Except the milk never seems to turn into butter. But you keep hoping, you know, I think I bought the dream like everyone else. I got hooked when I was a kid. I remember when *West Side Story* came out in Paris, I was ten or something, I wanted to see that movie so bad, I didn't have enough money to buy the ticket, but I had to go and see it, it was a matter of life and death, my whole life depended on seeing Natalie Wood shout America, America in front of a sordid tenement, so I went anyway with my girlfriend and I sold some stamps that I had in my wallet at the door of the theater but that still didn't do it, so I ended up panhandling until I had enough money to get in.

Lulu gets up and kicks her heels, lifting her thin legs in black long johns high up to her chin, shaking her shoulders.

New York, New York, what a wonderful town!

When Lulu leaves, Salvine pulls down the shades, as Julian had suggested, changes into a long flowing robe of moonstone-colored satin and unplugs her phones. She feels she's coming into one of these periods when she has to close off the outside world and descend into herself. She wonders if Lulu's visit has precipitated that mood.

Salvine needs to exist in secret. Her soul blossoms in high-perched penthouses, far from indiscreet gazes, buried under morning glories, in hollowed-out townhouses with wide-open, restructured volumes, on glossy maple floors covered with Oriental carpets, on mezzanines with a sculptured banister overlooking a central foyer furnished with Victorian divans, in five-thousand-square-feet lofts under skylights, with a patio in the middle and a fountain springing out of a plaster cherub's mouth. She has to have secret gardens. Low and hidden doors, whose key she is the only one to hold. She sometimes remains for days without leaving her house, subsisting on tea, milk, various whole wheat breads and sharp cheddar, consulting the Tarot until it turns favorable.

She calls that *faire le vide,* emptying herself. She turns her answering machine on and stocks her fridge. Those days she needs a lot of milk. She says it's a regression to early childhood. She tunes in to the present. She hushes interferences, urban cacophony. Others go looking for green, she says. I don't need to go to the country. I go to my secret garden. Where the fountain springs, climbing plants thicken the walls. You're running away from yourself, her friends tell her. It is the eternal dilemma. She says she learns more that way than she would if she stayed on a war footing, and that the New York merry-go-round is more of an escape.

Lulu's visit was all she needed to sink into solitary confinement. To settle into it. Watching adamantine reflections. Lapis-lazuli veining. A dark green watered silk taffeta. The goal is to forget everything. To let go. But her dreams taste of war. Crowds loom in and out of them, crammed into trains, buses. She dreams of buses lined up along the sidewalk which are used as rendezvous and fucking spots for solitary souls in search of soul mates. You walk into the bus, waiting to catch somebody's gaze, you take up with him or her, or you try someplace else. The buses are crammed with strangers folded in each other's arms, entangled naked legs and feverish gazes searching for each other. They smell of rancid beer, of sweat, of sperm. It feels as if dams have broken down, as if it is the game of the last chance. You go from bus to bus pursuing glowing eyes or a sensual lip or a turned-up breast glimpsed at behind a clouded window. As if sensuality becomes stronger as despair gets closer.

Halloween night in Hell

It's Halloween Night in Hell. It doesn't say Hell on the facade. It doesn't say anything. It looks just like another abandoned building, crumbling away to the core. An old awning juts out, desolate, its scalloped edges eroded by decades of rain and snow, a myriad of little bulbs hanging from under it, long dead, the wires partially pulled out, dried out underbelly left untouched, along with the verdigrised Art Deco brasswork on the glass doors. Inside it's dark. Dark like the huge ballrooms of a decrepit castle dimly lit with candles whose flickering flames can't reach its deeper recesses. The walls have been painted black over the peeling paint, over the elaborate moldings running along the baseboards, edging the ceiling and circling the heavy crystal chandeliers, over the tin ceilings. Long mirrors, their silvering scratched and tarnished, their gilding faded, hang from thick cords at an angle from the walls, multiplying the costumed crowd from side to side. There are a few tables in the deep downstairs foyer, and old chairs upholstered in black-and-white fake leopard-skin plastic, remnants of a distant past when this place used to be a Yiddish movie theater doubling as a dance hall for the Jewish community on Sunday afternoons. The gold has faded, the velvet is worn, but because nothing has been added or replaced, the ghosts from the past haven't been disturbed and mix freely among the crowd or lurk in the balcony.

Upstairs the wooden floor creaks under the weight of the crowd. White candles perched on tall silver candlesticks stand on the tables hemming the dance floor. Groups of strange characters sit at the tables, watching the dancers throw their coats and jackets at their feet to swing and twirl more freely. There are men in drag, powdered and rouged, in multilayered muslin ballgowns and beehives, fluttering their two-inch-long eyelashes and straightening their rhinestone-rimmed butterfly glasses with heavily manicured hands, and straight men in straight masculine woolen skirts worn with cotton socks and black army boots. There are cowgirls flaunting the fringes of their suede jackets and kicking their heavy-duty snakeskin boots, and devils sporting short red horns on their foreheads and impertinent tails curling out of their pants, and slender women with pencil moustaches squaring their thin shoulders in oversized suits, and survivors of a nuclear holocaust, their limbs horribly burnt, strange alien hair sprouting out of their bruised skulls, their tattered clothes glued with dried blood. There are big hunky fellows in diapers tightly wrapped under their naked potbellies, sucking on baby bottles full of vodka, there is a girl dressed as a Tylenol tablet dancing with an Advil girl and a serious older man sandwiched between signs saying COSTUME stapled to his chest and his back and a black man whose T-shirt and tights seem to have been run through a shredding machine and whose hair is crawling with live maggots rushing in and out of a rotting piece of meat attached behind his ear.

Yuk, Lulu yells over the music, attempting to show the man with the maggots to Mystique, Andrée and Sirouelle with whom she is sitting at a table. Look at this guy! How repulsive, the three of them yell back. They've just come over from the Village parade, mingling with the costumed crowd, dancing and chanting in the streets, throwing confetti on the onlookers, ending up for dinner in a little Italian restaurant where the waiters surrounded them with eager hands wandering around their shoulders and their waists. Mystique is sporting an extravagant pillbox hat sitting at a dangerous angle on her hair, a long purple feather standing upright preceding her like a figurehead, and her body is encased in a fake leather, skintight strapless gown curving around her hips and constricting her knees—my fantasy of sexy, she laughs, sauntering to get to the dance floor. Lulu is dressed as an old-fashioned bride from the time when there were still real brides, all in white lace—my fantasy, she says, a real wedding gown, virginity, going all the way, long veil down to the waist and covering the face, train long enough to gather on the arm . . . Andrée and Sirouelle are twin George Sands, in black tuxes, starched pleated shirtfronts, cigarette holders—our fantasy, they whisper to each other, dancing cheek-to-cheek, *les yeux dans les yeux.*

The last group of trick-or-treating children have long gone home, carrying their plastic shopping bags full of sticky sweets and candy bars and cheap cookies and occasional apples stuffed with razorblades. They've wiped their small faces clean of the cat's moustache or the princess's rouge or pulled off a Gobot's menacing mask. They're sleeping on their narrow cots, their hands joined under their cheeks, their teeth gently rotting in sugars, their dreams full of violent nightmares, of giant turtles taking over their parents' place, of wicked witches of the west riding a giant broom flying in through the half-open window.

In Hell, a girl dressed as a butterfly is hanging from the huge crystal chandelier above the dance floor, flying up and down attached to an invisible wire, flapping her arms wrapped in gauze like fluttering wings.

On the balcony floor there is a succession of various anterooms which connect with narrow, dark stairs leading to a side street. The first one is lit up with black light which makes you look violet, the only decor being a busted tv screen painted over with a stylized Western scene in black and white ink. The room serves as a powder room with a row of toilet stalls at the end. In the far corner a girl in white-turned-purple is having her left palm read by a man with a grey goatee. A door ajar reveals another girl in party dress sitting on the john, her skinny body folded over, her long hair hanging over her knees, one leg spread to the side, a silver pump dangling from her toes. Lulu touches her shoulder. The girl doesn't answer. Lulu shakes her a little. The girl moans. She is okay, she says. Her lace train sweeping behind her, Lulu crosses the next room whose tin walls and ceiling, of gold dabbed with red, are speckled with mirrors, most of them standing on the floor and only reflecting feet and legs. She's staring at a pair of heavy black boots strapped with a metal chain, when a voice comes from above, saying Lulu in a familiar ironical tone, and her gaze travels up from the boots, up the long black overcoat, the white shirt tied in a silk lavallière, up the pale skin and the faded freckles, the plump dark mouth, the slight sneer at the corner of the lips, up the hair dyed black with the reddish-blond roots showing, curling under a tall silky *haut-de-forme* that Julian takes off, bowing formally before her. Would you like to dance, he asks. She's startled. Last time she saw him he was burning himself out with heroin. There is a glow in his skin now, a light in his eyes that doesn't seem dimmed by the glassy torpor of the drug. She feels pulled like a stretched rubber band, like she did when she first met him. No, she says, I don't want to dance. Watching his skinny white hands clutch a pair of butter-colored gloves. They move through groups of people checking their costumes, freshening their makeup, whispering some gossip and giggling, sniffing white powder from tiny silver spoons. They walk from room to room, ending up alone in a low-ceiling garret furnished with a couch upholstered in sparkling purple vinyl. We could be going to our wedding, Lulu remarks. We could be exchanging rings right this minute in front of an altar. Yes, he says. I never thought you could be so . . . virginal.

COP KNIFED IN HALLOWEEN RAMPAGE

A twenty-two-year-old off-duty police officer was stabbed by one of fifteen to twenty costumed youths while he was jogging on Staten Island. A youth wearing a black mask and costume sprayed the officer with a fire extinguisher. When the officer confronted the teenager, other costumed members of the gang jumped him and dragged him to the ground, where he was stabbed by one of them.

There are spiderwebs nested in the corners of the windowsills, cockroaches rushing out from between the knives and forks in the cabinet drawers, running at the bottom of the old bathtub, in the clothes Tillie pulls out of her big plastic bags in the middle of Halloween night, searching for a long flowered dress and a flowered parasol and a pastel straw picture-hat to dress up as a lady-in-waiting at a garden party of the Royal Court of England. She shakes the clothes. They are full of cockroaches which drop with a tiny, flat sound, scurrying for cover with an unerring instinct to avoid the tip of the shoe, the rolled newspaper Tillie threatens them with.

Julian tells her he's trying to keep his habit under control, that he's been doing poetry performances. He calls himself the Mad Poet, or the Wild Poet. He says New York is coming into a new romantic age. Look at you: isn't that costume a yearning for romanticism? I thought it was ironical, she says. He says irony is also paying homage. Maybe we could call it cynical romanticism, or nihilistic romanticism. But all she cares about is to feel the rubber band stretch, stretch, stretch, and then snap. The intensity of her desire burns and liquifies and propels her beyond the threshold of reality. You know, he says, his hands slowly, maddeningly creeping along her ankles, her neck, her shoulders, you're taking me someplace even drugs can't take me. They lie on the couch amidst Lulu's lace skirt and petticoats, looking for all the world like lovers in a passionate embrace, only he's inside of her, making her come secretly as strangers stream by throwing them a bored look.

A navy-blue limo slides in front of the entrance to Hell, dropping Salvine in a high-style red suit, long straight skirt, leg-o'-mutton sleeves slashed with fake astrakhan fur, red toque, two friends in tow. Salvine negotiates with the doorman because she's supposed to be on the guest list and he can't find her name, then negotiates through the crowd.

This is a marriage made in Hell, Julian whispers as he bends to kiss Lulu through the veil shading her face.

Had we planned it, it couldn't have been better.

Now you know what it's like to marry as a virgin and die in ecstasy in your husband's arms.

What arrogance! I want more. I want you to unbutton every button of this dress and uncover every layer of lace and silk and see the exquisite white body no man has ever laid eyes upon. I want to see a man's member for the first time, rising stiff and purple out of the fly of a proper tuxedo.

How would you know?

How would I know what?

That it was stiff and purple?

I looked.

No. You had your chaste gaze lost in my amorous eyes.

Unbeknownst to you I lowered my chaste gaze toward your secret weapon and checked the merchandise. I may have been a virgin but I ain't no fool.

And what did you think?

As a first-time bride I'd say it felt better than it looked.

Salvine sails through the crowd, nodding to acquaintances on her way to the dance floor and the bar where she picks up drinks for herself and her friends. You seem quite at home here, one of her friends says. I've known the owner for a long time, she says. I think he is upstairs, I'd like to say hello. What a crowd! Let's take the back stairs. It'll be easier.

When they emerge at the door closing the top of the stairs, all they see is the mass of white and black, white lace and the white crown of orange blossoms from which hangs the white veil, the black overcoat and the black *haut-de-forme* lying on the floor. Then Julian catches Salvine's eyes and he freezes. What, says Lulu, confused, sensing the change in him. She sits up and sees Salvine at the door.

Salvine! *Ça alors. Pour une surprise* . . . She gets up to hug Salvine who stops cold looking at Julian. I didn't know you two knew each other, she says in English while Julian makes a little ironic bow before her, pressing his *haut-de-forme* to his heart and bringing her hand to his lips. She yanks her hand out of his while her friends and Lulu watch without understanding.

Comme le monde est petit, says Lulu.

Very small indeed, Salvine adds, now all sweet smiles, introducing everyone, then offering to go back to the dance floor for more drinks.

Julian is nervous as he readjusts his hat and pulls his soft suede gloves on. Instantly Lulu knows Salvine and he have been lovers, maybe still are. But Salvine moves her thin fingers loaded with rings around her waist, whispering in her ear in French that she feels as if she was marrying off her daughter, and they giggle like two best friends checking out people's costumes.

Downstairs the live band has started to play, it's a small hot band from Britain that believes that louder is better and threatens to crash the sound system. People are standing up thirty rows deep in front of the stage trying to catch a sight of the lead singer in a brocade suit tangoing with the mike, but what most of them only manage to glimpse is the spiked hair rising like a black sun from the woman drummer's head and undulating with her lethal attacks on the percussion. Great, yells Mystique, leaving Andrée and Sirouelle behind at the table and moving forward toward the deafening sound pouring out of the barrage of huge loudspeakers pulsating under the ceiling. At the foot of the stage there's a boy in a leather suit who thinks she's too much and instantly feels intense lust for her round shoulders and cleavage blossoming out of her heart-shaped mermaid sheath. He loves the long fake braid hitting the small of her back in a suggestive curl and he dances his way next to her.

Où as-tu rencontré Julian? How do you know Julian? Salvine asks Lulu casually as they are both leaning against the downstairs bar in the relatively quiet foyer, the music slightly muffled on the floor below. Lulu says she met him a year ago at a party, perceiving a proprietary interest behind Salvine's offhanded question. She tries to remember if Julian ever mentioned an older woman or a rich woman or parties he might have gone to uptown but Julian never talks about the people he knows and very little about himself. She realizes she knows nothing about him except what she guesses about his life in the bars and clubs, what he calls his refusal to acknowledge the gender barrier, but he doesn't acknowledge any barriers, and certainly not barriers as mundane as the age or the social barrier, on the contrary he loves to straddle worlds and appears with a white tuxedo jacket at an uptown dinner with the same ease as he walks back from the West Side bars, wasted, with his heavy work boots and his biker's leather jacket. I like boys, he says, which doesn't mean that I don't love women. And I mean women, not girls. She often wondered where he got the money for his clothes, impeccably cut antique jackets and good leather, worn down and seasoned, usually secondhand but you could tell they hadn't been picked up at the Salvation Army either. Salvine and Lulu finger their glasses pensively, letting go of a conversation they both feel might be loaded with potential bullets. Julian has disappeared. There is no trace of his thin silhouette even as the crowd thins out by waves, groups of people trying unsuccessfully to hail cabs in this forsaken part of town in order to join other parties or move on to other clubs. Lulu sees Mystique getting her coat and leaving with an unknown young man of attractive features and doesn't attempt to call her.

The band has stopped playing, hardcore clubgoers replacing

little by little the Halloween crowd. The butterfly girl has abandoned her wings behind her, they flutter under the chandelier having lost their body like the Cheshire Cat's smile. Lulu makes a last round in the back rooms. Three girls are sitting on the sparkling purple couch, quiet and bored. The low mirrors in the red-speckled gold room only reflect tired feet and uninteresting boots.

Alone on Houston Street, his hands thrust deep in his overcoat pockets, Julian walks in long strides, fighting against the sharp wind eddying from downtown. He's not trying to get a cab. He's tucked his tall hat under his arm and keeps walking across town. The street people at the corner of the Bowery have let the garbage can fires burn out and run to a shelter, only a couple of bodies are still huddled under a heap of clothes and newspapers tucked along a fence. The windshield cleaning team is long gone and the few cars roller-coasting along Houston's potholes stop unbothered at the Broadway crossroad. Julian keeps walking west, past Sixth Avenue, past the Village, all the way to the Hudson River docks where the streets run dark and empty, except for occasional groups of men dressed in leather regalia spilling out of smoky storefronts. Julian puts his *haut-de-forme* on and smoothes his gloves and pushes the metal door, pausing a moment before entering the overheated, crowded bar.

Life was dark

I kept looking for my mother. There was a trunk at my aunt's house full of clothes that had belonged to her, and some photographs in a cardboard box next to a Chesterfield cigarette case in metal still giving out the gingerbread aroma of blond tobacco. An old sewing kit in a wicker basket with a collection of odd buttons, vintage '45. There were miniature Croix-de-Lorraine buttons and Lucky Strike buttons, a tiny enamel version of the pack of cigarettes so popular during World War II. The trunk had a faint smell of moth balls and mildewed cardboard and dusty fabrics. I tried on her silk slips and cambric camisoles, they were a little big for me, I imagined the fabric stretched on her full breasts like a second, tight skin, but on me they drooped sadly. I sniffed for her perfume but the smell of time was over-whelming. Once when I was alone in the house I got dressed up in her clothes, an ivory slip under an unmatched straight woollen skirt and suit jacket with black velvet lapels, cinched at the waist, a pair of platform shoes and a black felt toque with a short perky voilette eaten up by the moths. Looking at myself in a mirror with an American cigarette between my gloved fingers that I pretended to pull out of the Chesterfield case, blowing the sweet smoke in round blue whirls, stretching my calves hosed in sheer nylon under the slit easing the tight skirt, I saw a young woman at the end of the war. It is six o'clock on a dark winter late afternoon, she's meeting an American soldier with clear blue eyes and square jaw at a Champs-Elysées café. Her family thinks she is spending the evening at her cousin's apartment near the Parc Monceau. Her lips are of deep cherry and her eyes made up charcoal black. They're drinking whiskey and soda at a small round table tucked behind the bar. His short blond crewcut makes her think of porcupine's bristle as their fingers intertwine between the glasses. He lifts up the veil to kiss her lips, eager to taste the red of her mouth. She responds to him, all her senses aroused, burning for him, but a part of her is detached, observes the scene with cool distance, a part which died when David, her Jewish lover, left for Treblinka.

I had invented a life for her, built of bits and pieces of information I had gleaned here and there. David was a mystery for me. I had read his name only two or three times in faded letters stashed away in the sitting-room dresser. It was a mere allusion in each case. But it seemed to me this name and the context in which it was written brimmed with forbidden passion and a sense of doom.

The CUCHIF ITOS sign blinks across the street. Lulu watches it as she lifts her eyes from the pad on which she has been feverishly scribbling, chewing on her pen, her mind wandering from her writing to Julian in her arms on Halloween night, to Salvine's eyes when she saw them together. There is a smell of cold tobacco in the air, unpleasantly mixing with that of oily fried eggs coming from the floor below, and of her own still warm coffee in a mug by her bed.

· · · ·

It's 11:05, purrs a voice on the radio. WINS News Time. You give us twenty minutes and we give you the world. It's windy and cold with snow flurries tonight. High thirty-five. Winds eight miles per hour... and more than one million Medicare elderly eligible in the city of New York... The hearings began this morning at 9:30... When the President meets the Belgian Prime Minister Martens, who faces re-election... is under considerable pressure to display deployment of MX missiles... Matter of shared risk, shared responsibility... Danger of mixing alcohol and gasoline.

WINS News Time 11:09. The WINS Accuweatherforecast. Low tonight twenty-four.

She sees Salvine standing against a door, her body sheathed in a black satin dress, her bare shoulders gleaming in the dim light of the *pâte-de-verre* Art Deco torches keeping watch in the hallway leading to her bedroom. Julian appears next, his hands burning for her. She smells of Shalimar, a sweet heady scent that has become for him the very smell of her, he is hungry for her heavy breasts, for her fleshy thighs, his wiry body twists around hers. She is a column offered to his gaze, to his touch. He peels the top of her dress down, revealing the globes of her white breasts. He presses her to him, playing with her till she moans, burying his face into the tissue going soft, delicately veined with purple lines, ripe, yielding to the touch, the nipples large and dark contrasting with the pearliness of the skin. Lulu sees them from behind, Julian's pulled her skirt up her ass, wide and soft too, he kneads it with his hands, his nails reach for the crack. I like real women, he's once said to Lulu, fe-males, women who've lived, whose flesh taste of past lovers and passion. He stiffens against Salvine. He wants the female to envelop him, to suck him in. I like to feel lost in a woman, he says. I like to lose it all. Salvine's hands are gloved in leather studded with rhinestones. She ties a satin ribbon around Julian's neck and wraps his wrists in leather behind his back. Julian's cock rises tender and exposed above his naked thighs. Lulu rolls around on her bed, making herself come time and again to that scene. Salvine's breasts hang over her unzipped dress. She licks him and hits him across the sex, rushing him then slowing him down on the verge of coming. Lulu closes up on his lips opening to a scream.

She gets up, fills a tea kettle with water and goes to the window to water the rubber plant curving next to the kitchen table. *La salope.* The bitch. While she, Lulu, sat down week after week in that penthouse, opening her soul to her, her memories. Stupid memories that keep pouring out of her which became these . . . things when she brought them to Salvine. Bits of herself she just gave away to be consumed by her. Just like Salvine must have consumed Julian, paying him like she was paying Lulu, his pound of flesh.

New York Air offers ninety-nine flights to Washington. Nobody does it better . . . Milwaukee 119. College basketball . . . John McEnroe played some of the strongest tennis of his career in Madison Square Garden yesterday . . .
      1010 WINS News Time 11:17.

Something she noticed, when she first arrived in New York, is the holes. The gaping holes. Now, she wondered, what holes? Imagining New York as a polka dot or a Swiss cheese city. No, not that kind of hole. She pursues holes in her mind, looking for one solid hole that yet keeps eluding her, she can only see the gaping windows of an abandoned tenement staring at her from the other side of the street. These are not holes. What about the grey smoke twirling above the pavement? Isn't it slipping out of some hole? And the cracks in the asphalt, between the bricks, in the sidewalks, through which plants grow in the springtime? And the potholes pockmarking the avenues?

Waiting for the right deal for the VCR you want? RCA 900 operates . . . Up to eight reading programs. Five heads for optimum quality. Great one-hundred-dollar rebate. But hurry! Offer expires February 1 . . . Now, at your participating RCA dealers.
      WINS News Time 11:22.

. . .

It was dark. There was a sense of perpetual darkness. Life wasn't radiant and spitfiring, it was deep muddy waters slowly flowing under concrete slabs, often eddying around entangled masses of weeds, obsessions swirling like twigs sucked in a vortex. Life had the intensity and surrealism of a dream. It was distorted faces as if photographed through a wide-angle lens coming at you with thick lips and stretched-out eyes. The faces closed in on you threateningly, their stares pinning you like a dead butterfly in a natural history museum case. I was a hole at the center of the vortex. If the twigs stopped twirling and the obsessions went away I knew there would be nothing left. It was the same later with Raphael. If he was removed from my life, if his weight was lifted off my chest, I thought I would soar like a helium-filled balloon breaking loose from a kid's wrist. His smothering presence was what kept me grounded. Without it I could have flown over the mountains or sunk deep in the ocean and drowned.

New York turned out to be the reality, the body of my dream. It looked and felt like my most hellish nightmares, but also like the sweet ozone of my dreams.

And the funny thing is: life stopped being terrifying.

She pauses again. Salvine won't see any of this. Not any more. What does she care anyway?

Raphael would turn me around and finger me. He'd spread me out with his thumb and tell me how exciting I looked. He tried to force his way in but when I pushed him away he cursed me and said his new girlfriend loved to do it that way. The day I left him, I felt so high with adrenaline I thought I would faint. I threw in my clothes and my books and the few things I had brought to his place, jewels and an antique casket and a photograph of my mother as a very young woman in an oval frame. I threw all my possessions in a big heap in the living room and tossed them in my suitcase until things started to spill out. Whatever didn't fit I left behind right in the middle of the carpet. I sat on the suitcase, bouncing several times in order to buckle the strap. When I was finished I threw my keys on the table without a note and banged the apartment door behind me. It took Raphael days to locate me and call and ask me in a carefully casual voice, what's the matter with you? Couldn't you even say goodbye to me?

Marie shows up as Lulu recalls Julian inside of her under the billowing wedding dress on Halloween night. The tv is on while they make love, Mario'd been watching a football game and a movie must've started because her eyes drift toward a blond running for her life in a car graveyard pursued by an old Chevy truck determined to run her over and cornering her against heaps of scrap metal. Lulu finds herself wondering when the woman is going to be saved from the killer car as Mario passionately sucks her breasts, and when she feels more relief at the woman's rescue than at her own orgasm, she knows it's time to be on her own, so she asks Mario to leave. She tells him she wants to be alone, she's funny about that sometimes, she's just got to be alone. He has a bruised look on his face and refuses to kiss her before walking out the door and she feels guilty to let him down, but she goes back to Julian's pale skin and cynical sneer.

Julian is Salvine's lover, Lulu tells Mystique as they get ready for the show.
    How do you know?
    I could see it in their eyes.
    So? You have Mario and Henry. What's the big deal?
    It's different to know. To put a face and a body in your lover's bed. He'd dropped out of my life, you know. I was finished with him.
    So you thought . . .
    Now he's back to torture me. I'm obsessed with them.
    They pull on their fake fur coats for the go-go number.
    Julian is a dangerous type, Mystique says, adjusting the platinum wig to her eyebrows. Let me tell you about the guy I picked up on Halloween night. Another weirdo . . .

Lulu meets Henry on the sixty-second floor

Meet me on the sixty-second floor, Henry tells her. It's a music people party. Music business. Boring. We won't stay long. Have a drink or two, then cab home.

The party features Buster Poindexter and the Banshees of Blue and a number of young men strutting around in pleated pants tapered at the ankle worn with white and black wing-tip shoes and layered hair spiked up in front in a tamer version of downtown musicians'. Hot dogs are served in paper wrappers on the buffet table. A cardboard sign showing a frankfurter in glossy colors advertises 100% BEEF. NO PRESERVATIVES. KOSHER. It's so hopeless to think of the past, Lulu thinks, looking at the grid of glittering red and white dots down below. Like hanging onto a sinking ship. It gives way the moment you believe you've got hold of it. I'm helplessly muddled and confused, she says out loud and laughing to a bald man who looks at her with alarm, wondering whether she is trying to be funny, or is actually in the throes of a severe depression.

Lulu is dancing to the beat of a camped-up fifties rock 'n' roll song, dreaming of black Africa, the Sahara and the Amazon jungle all together when a middle-aged man with a fat belly protruding under his polo shirt twists his way next to her, jamming a bejeweled hand in her side. You shouldn't be dancing by yourself, he whispers in her ear, so close she feels his moist breath on her neck. I am not, she tells him, look at all these people around me, what do you think they're doing? Then Henry shows up, scanning the crowd, bristling with energy, looking like he just came back from the country, ruddy cheeks, tweed jacket, his beard overgrown. He grabs one of the 100% kosher hot dogs and washes it down with a Scotch on the rocks. Come on, he says, let me introduce you to some people and let's go. He runs his hand down Lulu's belly, stopping just short of her legs, smacking his lips in anticipated pleasure.

How is your fiancée? Lulu asks coldly.

Shhh! he says. Let's not talk about Sherry right now.

So you are really getting married, Lulu says, stretched naked in the middle of the reindeer fur spread over the floor.

Yup. We'll do it in the spring. Then I want to move out of here.

You don't mean leave New York?

The time's come, Lulu. You get burned out in this city. I want real nature. I see a big sprawling white house with clapboard siding somewhere in Maine or in Nova Scotia, huge spread along the ocean, hunting, fishing. I want to become a regular gentleman farmer, wear rubber boots, see my kids run around in the mud . . .

You're crazy.

No. I'll come to New York when I have a show. Or, you know (he winks at her), see my friends.

I'm sorry for Sherry, Lulu says.

Henry takes Lulu's hand and squeezes it between his.

We'll be very happy.

They've just made love in front of the huge mirror hanging

at the foot of Henry's bed, aroused by their reflection played on the wall, better than a porn flick, I've got to admit, Lulu said the first time they went up to his room, opening her legs to the mirror.

I love the taste of you, he says, licking his fingers as if he had caviar on them.

The night is black and wet, the lights on the Hudson and along the New Jersey shore shattered in red and green and silver splinters blurred by the rain, the tip of Manhattan vanishing in the fog. Once in a while the hoot of a ship throbs darkly across the river. Henry gets up to get a robe and a drink and stands next to Lulu watching the rain splattering in sudden gusts against the window.

You know, Lulu says, not turning back, why I don't get tired of New York, why I don't feel the need to run away from here, like from everywhere else I've lived?

I used to feel that way, Henry says, squatting behind her, wrapping one arm around her shoulder.

I see Manhattan like an ocean liner adrift in the middle of the Atlantic, never reaching its port. The moorings have been cast off. There's no turning back to dry land. We're all thrown together on this phantom ship, hallucinating, without connection to the other world. It's a trip from which we'll never come back.

You're a romantic.

I didn't say it was a good trip.

You're a romantic all the same. I think anybody who leaves their country like we did—I'm not talking of the forced immigrations of the turn of the century that had primarily economical reasons—is a romantic: you have to believe in another world, you have to be passionate enough to break all your ties and start afresh. To want to make your own life and become your own hero. I supposed that's what I wanted when I came here. Build the life of my dream.

You think the first settlers were dreamers?

They were looking for economic outlets but I'm sure they dreamed of adventure. Settling on other continents was a great adventure for the white man. America is the only place where the white man fully realized his dream: to completely take over a continent.

It's weird. There's still a sense that things are up for grabs here, that nobody really has a birthright to own this place. But it's not up for grabs, really, right? I mean it's a myth. We're all like flies blinded by the lamp hanging on the porch. Or maybe the dead Indians' ghosts are reclaiming the land.

Aren't you getting cold?

No. I like to sit by the window and imagine the sea. Henry, I can't believe what you're doing.

You'll come and visit us up in Maine.

Gimme a break.

Henry lies down at Lulu's feet on the rug. His cock is hard again. She strokes it absentmindedly, feeling the bulge thicken inside her palm.

I've been doing some choreography. You want to see?

No. All I want to see is your tight little cunt dripping with juices. Here, he says. See: I can't wait.

She aches for Julian. He's stayed away from her since Halloween night. Salvine called her once or twice but Lulu said she was very busy and postponed their meetings.

Mystique, I know they're lovers. If you'd seen her eyes.

What about Mario?

He went home to Puerto Rico to see his grandmother who's dying.

Something old, something new, something borrowed, something blue.

I can't believe people still get married in this day and age, Lulu says. I hate love stories.

One has nothing to do with the other, Mystique says.

The year seems to take forever to die. The slowness of these hours under a grey sky bloated with imminent snow, gutters muddy from slush. It's New Year's Eve and it promises to be dull. Somebody said something about the pathos, the sadness of Russians and Eastern Europeans. Because they've been through the Gulag or because of the Slavic soul? It is so chic to be a Russian émigré or Eastern European refugee in New York, sighs Mystique, looking at herself to read her feelings. Or just a plain European. Not a Midwesterner like myself. From O-hi-o. Looking hard at the mirror. Through the mirror. Is there a person there?

The day is fading into the grey-blues and there's nobody in the world that Mystique would really want to speak to. She used to explain the rest of the world's indifference and neglect by a pimple growing on her nose. Now she attributes it to her lack of persistence, or drive, or aggressiveness. Then, pushing it a bit further, to her paranoia. Coming full circle. That's what they mean when they say in America you hold yourself responsible for your fate. Impossible even to take refuge behind a pimple or bad luck. Bad luck! Touch wood. Quick! Cross your fingers. Bad word. How dare you? No such thing as bad luck. You precipitated it with your negative moods.

Somebody calls, an old friend of an ex-lover, to wish Mystique a Happy New Year. He's worked all day and the previous nights on closing financial deals. He sounds real excited about it and thinks he's made a lot of money. Mystique says she is dancing at the club and would rather stay home by herself. He says after all the pressures from work, do I need the pressure to have fun and get drunk?

She toys with the idea of unplugging the phone. Going to bed at nine. Could use the sleep. Good for the circles under the eyes. Good for the complexion. She would just quit cold. Not show up. Not even call Marty up. Split tomorrow morning for a warm country. Far far away. But she picks up her bag and heads for the Blue Night Lounge.

Dinner is set in Salvine's living room on a small table. Two flowered plates, crystal glasses on high stems, two silver candlesticks with red candles, oysters on a bed of ice laid at the bottom of a silver platter, Champagne in a bucket set on a tripod near the table, canapés of Scottish salmon and black caviar on a coffee table between the divans.

Salvine waits, her long velvet dress opened deep between her breasts and raised at the back in a high collar around her nape, a blue orchid at the waist, long rhinestone earrings framing her neck. She smokes Russian cigarettes with a gold tip that she puts out halfway down and stares at the illuminated city.

The doorbell rings. Julian walks in in his old black tuxedo, the same one he was wearing on Halloween night, looking tired, dark circles under his eyes, his skin drawn, greyish over the sharp cheekbones.

You're late, Julian.

I'm sorry, he says, bending to kiss her.

She uncorks the bottle of Champagne, hands him a glass, raises hers.

Happy New Year!

Happy New Year, Salvine . . .

They sit down on one of the divans, Julian starts wolfing down a few canapés, apologizing, saying he hasn't eaten all day. Salvine looks at him coldly, playing with a small gold lighter on the marble table. They make small talk over the appetizers, small talk over the oysters after they move to the table. Just the way we eat them in France, Salvine remarks. Unwashed, tasting strongly of the ocean, thick and slippery under the tongue, a dash of lemon. Julian says they are delicious, he never had such good oysters.

What exactly is your relationship with Lulu? Salvine asks.

Julian swallows his oyster, has a long drink from his glass, takes his time.

You have long-delayed reactions. Why are you asking me now?

I wanted to see for myself, see what your attitude would be.

I had stopped seeing her. We bumped into each other at Halloween.

Bumped into. So to speak.

So to speak.

So it was her this summer. It was her all along.

It was her.

What a coincidence, *hein?*

Julian wipes his mouth with the pink linen napkin, drops it angrily by his plate.

You don't own me. Yet. You can't control my relationships.

No, my dear. I wouldn't dream of doing that. But it was a little obvious, wouldn't you say?

I thought you were cool.

Are you still seeing her?

Julian gets up to take one of her Russian cigarettes on the coffee table, lights it up, walks to the fireplace, his back to the burning logs.

Salvine, I think you're going too far.

She gets up too, carrying her Champagne to the window, looking at the dark hole of the park.

Maybe you're right, she says. Maybe this place should be underground, a secret cavern whose entrance would be covered with moss, maybe at the foot of the Reservoir. You know, Julian, I could go much further than that. And if I am not mistaken, you need me more than I need you.

Is that a threat?

No. It's a fact.

Intense light from the high blue sky burns Salvine's eyes tired from a night of partying. 7:30 A.M. the first of January the phone rings and Salvine extends her hand toward the receiver, knocking Julian's chin in her move, excuse me, she says, thinking, the sky's really cleared up, the temperature must've dropped, New York dawns can be so beautiful. Hello, she says, oh, *maman, tu sais quelle heure il est? C'est le jour de l'an, quand même* . . . You know what time it is? It's New Year's Day . . .

In France an old woman shrivels away, a ghost floating in a small cottage at the outskirts of Poitiers, with a nursemaid who cooks her meals, gives her her medications and her baths, cleans up her bed and fusses about her moods. An old and respectable matriarch she had hoped to become. Instead fading away. Her son visits her out of filial duty. Her daughter has left many years ago for America. She's bitter. Sometimes there is humor and fleeting tenderness. She turns her back to it, indulging in her children's rejection. As if deep down, she'd known all along, since she was herself a child . . . Trembling with rage she accuses her maid of robbing her. The maid, feeling wronged, defends herself, tries to keep her cool. She needs the job and she knows the old girl is losing her marbles. The old lady calls her son on the phone to complain that her jewelry has been stolen and her food is being slowly poisoned. *Bonne année, maman,* the son says, appeasing, promising to stop by. She breaks into tears. Nobody understands her. They're all out to get her.

It is 7:30, New Year's morning. I hear your mother passed away, the old lady tells Salvine on the phone, in a broken voice. I heard she was dead, I am sorry. This must have been quite a blow for you. *Bonne année, maman,* Salvine says. How are you feeling? Is the nurse with you? Let me talk to her.

Who was it? Julian asks, half-asleep.

My mother. She was calling from France to wish me a Happy New Year.

At this time?

She didn't remember about the time difference.

Salvine's father once told her, it's not dying I am afraid of, but getting old. Having to let go of the young man I once was. I still think I am. I thought I would always be. When you're young you think you're immortal. Too much narcissism makes you dread age and death even more. It was a few months before she left for New York. She never got a chance to see him again, young or old. He died from cirrhosis of the liver a year later.

My father was lucky, she says to Julian, playing with his funny strand of hair sticking up.

Why?

He died before it was too late.

She looks at the sky. Pure blue from her bed. Not a building in sight, not even a tree. The pure cloudless unpolluted azure of a razor-sharp cold morning.

Make love to me, she says, wrapping her arms around Julian.

But as his hand reaches between her legs, she keeps staring into the blue.

Myra Schneider

Winter was back and with it the taste of Blistex on the lips and the crispness of the air that makes the skin alive with a red flush and too dry around the jaw and the ears. The sky rose high and periwinkle blue over the sharp skyline glittering like a jeweled crown beyond the East River as Myra Schneider drove over the Kosciusko Bridge on her way back to Manhattan. Her car was all shiny green paint and chromes, and she always drove it with the roof down, no matter how low the mercury dropped. She was coming back from visiting her son in a private-care house for the mentally retarded and past the rows of tenements and industrial lofts all she could see was the image of a twenty-five-year-old young man with globulous eyes and a neck that seemed too soft to carry the load of his oversized head.

That was the day Lulu saw her for the first time. At that point she was driving down Fifth Avenue in a dark green 1956 Oldsmobile convertible with the roof down, aviator's glasses shielding her eyes, a black woolen scarf draped as a turban around her head, her silvery-blond hair whipping in the wind. An apparition in sub-freezing temperatures. Lulu just caught a glimpse of a strong Jewish nose below the glasses, and a mouth tightened by the cold.

Now she is sitting across the room from her, at Salvine's, on a deep couch, her thin body dressed in white leather up to the neck, her legs folded tight under her. A young man caters to her, bringing her drinks and sandwiches, making a big fuss about her. She wears a bracelet made of metallic rings that seems too heavy for her wrist.

It's Myra Schneider, haven't you heard of her? Julian tells Lulu, as she mentions the scene. He says she had been a well-known painter, but had fallen out of favor. She had been a dancer too, but something had happened to her. Now she lives a withdrawn, Greta Garbo–like existence, a star in hiding, and Julian doesn't think she's painting anymore. He says he had an affair with her years ago when he was eighteen and discovering life. Lulu doesn't believe him.

She still is so beautiful, don't you think? Salvine whispers to Lulu, sitting beside her. She's had a tragic life. Do you know about her son?

They didn't find out right away about Myra Schneider's son's disease. It was one of those rare cases when the baby looks perfectly normal at birth, the head maybe just a little bit larger than it should be, and they didn't pay much attention to that because Myra Schneider was young enough not to be in the high-risk mothers' group. Had the doctors spotted the condition right away, however, nothing more could have been done. When it became clear that her son was suffering from a form of Down's Syndrome, she and the child's father understood that the only hope to ameliorate his condition would be intensive mental and physical reeducation, or rather education which, at best, would bring the boy's IQ to about 65 but would not impart him with significant autonomy skills. His life expectancy, moreover, was twenty to thirty years, which one doctor said, infuriating Myra Schneider, was maybe for the best.

They voted for the MX missiles. Germany voted for the Pershing missiles. In interviews liberal artists and writers are quoted saying a worldwide holocaust is down the road. Someone says it would be a relief to blow ourselves up, because we are heading toward self-destruction anyway and we can't stop ourselves. We are so tied up in our will to power and technological madness that total destruction is the only solution. Lulu imagines graffiti on the walls: THE ONLY SOLUTION: TOTAL DESTRUCTION! It is New Year's Day and they sip Champagne and nibble on petits fours by the huge Christmas tree set up in the middle of Salvine's penthouse. The lights are soft and rosy, everybody in dark colors and sleepy-eyed from partying until the wee hours of a freezing first of January dawn. World destruction seems eons away. Nobody dwells on the subject. Nobody dwells on any subject. Topics slip them by, washed away by lazy yawns.

Myra Schneider laughs unexpectedly and leans toward Salvine. Do you remember the Morrises? she says. She has a deep voice, veiled, almost a man's voice.

Why yes, of course, Salvine says. What on earth made you think of them?

I had a vision of the house on Barrow, and Laura Morris walking down the front steps in an evening gown holding arms with Hermione in her dashing cashmere man's suit, walking into the Morrises' vanilla-and-chocolate Chrysler (did they still have it when you met them?) for a night on the town presumably destined to end in Hermione's bed, while Morris, in shirtsleeves, his tie undone, was staring at them, speechless at the door.

Yes. I remember the scene very well. When he got back in, he walked right to the bar and got blasted in a few minutes, draining tumblers of Scotch one after the other until he collapsed from the barstool. What a scene. But they stayed together for at least ten years after that, while she ran the steamiest lesbian affairs in town. I think Laura had nostalgia for the thirties, for Montparnasse in the thirties to be precise. Or Prohibition time. Instead it was McCarthy and pretty housewives with lacquered short curls and wasp-thin waists trying out their new washing machines. Laura's flamboyance really stirred the blood. I think that's why he stayed with her, in spite of everything, don't you think? Anyway what made you think of her?

I thought I saw her the other day. If it was her she hadn't kept much of her past flamboyance. It was a bag-lady sitting on a couch on Second Avenue.

Salvine stays silent for a moment. I haven't heard from her in a long time, she says. I wonder what happened to her.

MAN KIDNAPS AND TORTURES HOMELESS WOMAN

A Manhattan building superintendent kidnapped and tortured a seventy-two-year-old homeless woman and held her prisoner in his apartment for about one month.

He reportedly tortured her and beat her with a wooden cane, blackening both her eyes, and bit her all over her body.

She really is a cat-lady rather than a bag-lady. She feeds about twenty stray cats. She has faded blue eyes, ex-blond hair, must've been beautiful in her youth, you can tell from the sharp bone structure and the straight nose, the tight quality of the skin, in spite of the damage caused by age and poverty. Grey coat. Little hat at an angle, sometimes with a feather. An interesting old-fashioned little hat, when you look at it closely. Arthritic fingers. Always polite. Not a bum. But lately, what with the food stamps cut and all, has taken to the soup kitchen. And this winter she's been seen begging around Second Avenue and the Bowery.

Outside it is five degrees below zero and no one wants to leave. It looks like they might end up spending the night on the velvet divans. Julian is lying on the carpet at Lulu's feet, his shoulder or his chin brushing against her leg as if by accident—he pulls away each time they touch.

Myra Schneider dances in front of Lulu. The theater is dark, the two red lights reading EXIT on either side of the stage bathe the front rows in a dark glow. She is Isadora Duncan with a white scarf wrapped three times around her neck and extended to the tips of her fingers. Her costume is in white chiffon, gathered around the waist. Her legs play a slow dance under the clear fabric, long shadows flowing in a perfect endless movement but without music.

A soft wind blows, lifting up the layers of chiffon, her scarf floats behind her. Myra Schneider drives her convertible, the wind is now fierce, Lulu is sitting next to her, the trees race past them with a buzz. Lulu knows Myra Schneider is going to die. Not Lulu though. She is sitting in the grass when the car hits the tree. The scarf is caught in the metal frame of the folded-down canvas roof. Lulu sees her gasp when her forehead hits the windshield, her neck snaps with the noise of a chicken bone cracking. The head going soft, a cloth doll thrown against the wheel. Blood from the bruises on her head gushing red on the immaculate fabric of her dress.

Myra Schneider is Isadora Duncan!

The words are out of her mouth, loud and clear, before Lulu knows she is pronouncing them. She is sitting up straight in a strange bed, with a dirty light coming from the wrong side of the room.

She is in Julian's bed. He grunts next to her, extends an arm to turn on the light.

What the hell . . .

She falls back on the pillow.

Nothing. Forget it. It was a dream.

This woman intrigues me. I find her so beautiful. No, not only that. As if untouched by age. The skin so tight. Eyes so clear . . .

Down at the club, Lulu watches Mystique remove her makeup

in the dressing room. As usual it stinks of warm beer and dirty feet. Mystique lights up a cigarette and crosses her ankles on the makeup table.

I heard she started as a dancer, I think it was during the war. She was supposed to have been extremely talented. Then she had an accident. She broke her leg or something and had to give up her career. That's when she got involved in painting.

I keep dreaming about her.

Julian and Salvine walk in Central Park under the snow. It falls crisp and light, quickly cushioning the grass hemming the alleys, alighting like tiny stars on their shoulders and hats and scarves. They walk around the Sheep Meadow and down the mall toward the Bethesda Fountain and across the lake through the little wood of bushes and winding alleys which is called the Ramble and up around the Reservoir where the snow falls thicker muffling the sounds of the city to quasi-silence. They barely talk, except things like, this snow is turning into a storm, or, have you ever been caught in a blizzard? And then they fall back into silence. Salvine, wrapped in an astrakhan coat and hat, seems determined to walk all the way to the other end of the continent, she wouldn't mind crossing the Great Lakes in sub-freezing temperatures, at least that's what Julian thinks, shivering in his threadbare overcoat, the collar turned up to his ears. I don't want to be naive . . . Salvine starts, suddenly breaking the silence. They've just reached a high point over the Reservoir. The whiteness of the park and the baroque turrets festooned with snow of the Central Park West apartment houses makes the whole thing look like an Andersen fairy tale filmed by Walt Disney. What you do in your life is none of my business, Salvine says, and I assume you've had other lovers, women and men, since we've known each other, but I don't want to see it in my house.

What do you mean?

Your little game with Lulu.

There was no game.

You left together last night, didn't you?

You jealous?

Men can be so cool. COOL. That's all you have in mind. Be on top of things. I'm not going to give you the pleasure of a scene.

So you're going to dismiss me. Thanks, but we don't need your services anymore. Do you give severance pay at least? Or do you fire your lovers without notice?

You were sitting at her feet the whole evening. You left with her. You did it out of spite.

It seems to me we already had this conversation two days ago. What's upsetting you about Lulu?

What do you do with her?

I beat her to death and stop only when she gets too bloody.

Salvine hits him with the back of her hand.

She's my friend. I don't want you to touch her.

Not everybody has the same taste as you, my dear.

I don't mean that. If you want it more plain: I don't want you to see her anymore.

Every decade, at her birthday, a year or two before hitting a round figure, Salvine goes through this crisis, thinking she has aged a hundred years, counting the new wrinkles, feeling her joints, and barely coming out of her bedroom. She thinks of Marilyn Monroe committing suicide at thirty-six. Saw the forty-year mark from afar. Looked once and stopped dead in her tracks. Couldn't throw herself into middle age. Not yet. Not yet. I am not ready, for God's sake! She remembers crying the evening before her twentieth birthday in Poitiers in the dead of winter, because she thought it was the end of her youth, she could see the years slip by her. She felt the same at twenty-seven, twenty-eight, thirty-nine . . . At nine, finding out she was nearsighted thinking she was doomed, she had focused her obsession on glasses, chastising herself with the sight of thirteen-year-old girls with huge visible eyes and twenty-twenty vision, with faces unmarred by a prosthesis. Now she is obsessed with the fine network of lines on her skin. She checks the puffiness under her eyes, selects the appropriate cream, taps it lightly around the eye area, sprays her face with a can of mineral water atomizer, cold from the fridge. Then she checks the slackness of the skin around her neck, thinking maybe the time has come for a facelift.

Julian's turned around without a word, his cold anger propelling him in quick jerky steps down the hill toward the north side of the park. Salvine watches him till the snow sucks up his skinny figure, wondering if he's going to score up in Harlem now that night is falling already, so early with Eastern Standard Time, what a shame, it steals so much daylight, they should call it Daylight Wasting Time, she gave him some money earlier, she knows he has these two tens with him, and he doesn't care about danger, it turns him on, he squeezes his blade in his pocket, one of these days they're going to find him dead on One Hundred-and-twelfth Street or down on Rivington or somewhere in Williamsburg shot or stabbed in the back and maybe that's what he's looking for, that's what he deserves he's so fucked up, but she knows he's going to come back to her sooner or later and she wonders why she can't just do a clean break like she usually does, what it is about him . . .

Salvine's
revenge

It's 5 A.M. on a cold snowy morning. Julian's letting himself into Salvine's apartment. He stumbles in the dark, tries to take off his shoes and grabs a candelabrum which topples on his leg. He limps through the foyer and hits an ashtray. Salvine finds him passed out on the settee. Blood trickles down from his side, gathering on the pale brocade to a dark stain. He hears her call an ambulance and stirs himself up. I am okay, he says. I got mugged by these assholes in the street. One of them stabbed me, he was so nervous with his fucking blade. But it didn't go deep, just through the flesh. Here, under the ribcage.

Where did that happen? Were you copping?

He sneers. Here, in your fucking Upper West Side neighborhood. Right after I got off the subway. I'll be okay. Please. I don't need an ambulance.

I'll go to the hospital with you. I want them to clean up the wound, make sure there is nothing wrong.

Julian's body is curled naked on the bed, his legs folded under him, his wrists attached to the brass posts with leather straps, his ass stretched out, white, the crack brownish/purplish with a few mousy hairs around the tight sphincter. Salvine's dressed in a black satin evening gown, strapless and tight around her waist and hips, with high pumps and long black mittens from which emerge her carmine fingernails. She's holding a white Argentine whip in her right hand and lashes at Julian's pale moon with gusto. She walks around the bed and showers the small of the back, the spine, the shoulder blades, down again. Julian moans. His back twists in pain trying to escape the blows. He manages to stretch his legs only to receive the full length of the whip across the back of his knees. Tiny drops of blood pearl on the surface of the skin, so pale, the freckles clustered on his shoulders are cut with red lines. His skinny body twists and roars. Please, he begs. Please. It's enough. Cold-bloodedly she works her way from the thighs to the heels, then the soles of his feet. He screams. Pleads. She drops the whip, only to light one of her Russian cigarettes, her red lipstick leaves a heart-shaped stain on the gold tip, she smokes the cigarette slowly, takes her time while he catches his breath. His eyes are covered with a blindfold, he turns his face to where he thinks she is, catching the sweet smell of tobacco, trying to figure out if his ordeal is over or if she's just taking a break.

Salvine wipes the blood from a cut on Julian's buttocks, then picks up the whip. Salvine, please, he whines. I can't take it anymore.
   What's the matter, my dear? Don't you love it? You love the pain, you say, or do you love it more when men do it to you?
   Salvine, you're going too far.
   The whip cracks sharp on his coccyx bone, rising a yelp from him.
   I want to hear you beg. I want to see you cry. I want to keep

going for such a long time that you'll start feeling the pains of withdrawal, but watch out: no puking on my silk sheets and my paisley pillows. Otherwise I'll throw you out and we'll never do this again that you like so much.

Salvine, I swear. It's too much.

The whip cracks and concentrates on the ass again, red and flushed.

I'm so sore. Please.

You're a clown. Take it like a man at least!

Why are you doing this?

Why are you doing what you do to me? Why are you torturing me all the time? When you find an answer to that, I'll tell you why.

What happened to your hard-on? Salvine asks. It's shrunk pitifully. It looks like a withered flower from the back. Shall we turn you around so that we can work on this problem? Maybe we can get it up again.

Why do you hate me so much?

I don't. I'm trying to give you pleasure. I'm sorry I am not succeeding any better. Maybe you like more sophisticated equipment.

I'll do anything you want. I'll suck you day and night.

That's what you say.

I swear.

You did it before. That's not enough.

I'll worship your body.

You're getting better.

Ouch, ouch.

Try again.

I'll worship you.

Warmer.

Ouch! I'll love you.

Warmer.

Tears run down his face, soaking the blindfold. The blows are getting lighter. Salvine's wrists are too sore for an efficient lash.

One should mechanize this, she says. Invent a whipping machine. Try again. If you find the word, I promise I'll stop. She manages to whip a mean blow that reaches the inside of his thighs.

Ahhh! I'll respect you.

ALL RIGHT! You know what, Julian. I think you can improve. I always knew you could make progress.

If dogs
had wings

If dogs had wings
and snakes had hair
and automobiles went flying through the air
if watermelons grew on huckleberry vines
we'd have more winter in the summertime

Turkey in the hay. Hay, hay, hay
turkey in the straw. Straw, straw, straw

Hit it up,
shake it up
any way at all
hit up a tune called turkey in the straw

Two little girls are singing and jumping on the sidewalk, holding hands. Their hair is braided in many short pigtails that bounce up and down all around their skulls.

we'd have more winter in the summertime

Hit it up
shake it up
any way at all
hit up a tune called turkey in the straw

They sing at full speed, the words stumbling over each other, then break up in giggles, embarrassed, burying their chins in the collars of their winter jackets, collapsing in more giggles against the fence as Lulu walks past them. They whisper to each other, their hands cupped around their mouths, their eyes rolling down to the ground. *Mira, mira, qué gordito,* they say pointing to a fat cat who's having trouble stretching himself flat to crawl under the fence. Then they resume their jumping.

If dogs had wings . . .

We played hopscotch, it was called *marelle,* with a flat pebble that landed in one of the numbered cases. There was hell at one end and paradise at the other and you had to jump a half turn whenever you hit one or the other end. Paradise was called *le ciel,* the sky, to go to the sky, *aller au ciel,* means to join *le petit Jésus* and the Virgin Mary and *Dieu le Père* sitting on his throne among the clouds with his long flowing white beard, in brief, the Holy Trinity all at once. We had a very Catholic hopscotch game. I went through all the motions, pumping the swing high all the way to the chestnut tree's lower leaves in the park, jumping two ropes, juggling with four balls, swinging the hula-hoop around my hips. Yet none of that got me acceptance in the little girls' society.

At the *botánica* where she buys her nickel candles, two green ones for money, two orange ones for success, four red ones for passion, Lulu sees a familiar back at the end of the rows of Virgin Marys and saints crowded on the shelves. Mario's leather jacket, his hands in his jeans back pockets, his white leather Pumas laced halfway up. He turns back, whistles Yo, man! He flashes his bright white smile in his dark face, swings his hips down the aisle, snapping his fingers.

Get down, Mario. Get down!

Yo! What you doing here?

Buying my good luck candles. When did you get back?

You believe in that bullshit? Theresa, he says to the owner behind the counter. This *gringa* believes in your fucking candles! Just came home, baby. Hey, good to see you!

You want to come light them with me?

Listen to this, Theresa. Do I want to go with her? Sure I'll light your candles, girl, sure.

Mario tells her his grandmother died on New Year's Eve, they all stayed with her day and night taking turns. Him and his mama and papi and his little brother and the priest held her hand the whole night until there was not a breath left in her. She let go just when dawn broke. There was this pink light piercing the darkness and the candles stretched long flames just for an instant, I swear to God, Lulu, the flames grew real long, it was as if they were celebrating her spirit breaking loose. She died with the first light of the first day of the year. Isn't that beautiful?

Lulu sees the little room in the ramshackle house, the candles flickering in the dark, the shadows moving around the room, somebody running to get some fresh water, pressing a wet handkerchief to the *abuela*'s parched lips, the low mumbling litanies of the priest reading from the Bible, Mario taking her hand to his heart when the soul leaves the tired body, at last liberated. She sees the turquoise sea licking the beach littered with coconuts, their fur wet from the night. She sees the fishing boats lying belly down below the wooden house, my grandfather was a fisherman, Mario says, she sees the shadows through the windows backlit by the long flames of the candles, so many candles, Mario says, you wouldn't believe, the room was full of candles, it was like a church, boy, the smell of wax, everybody brought a candle, family, friends, acquaintances, everybody in the village, she was very much loved, they all stopped by to say *adiós*, Lulu sees them moving behind the window, then the pink line of dawn emerges at the edge of the sea, where the water is crystal clear like an aquamarine stone, and the door cracks open, someone raises his arms to the sky as if letting go of a dove, the fingers stretched as if following the bird's flight and they all gather at the door to watch the red disk of the sun pop out of the ocean in one single leap, throwing long shadows across the beach. Lulu says, Mario, take me to your country. Take me to the Caribbean. Take me to a place where one believes in the soul, believes that the body is but an envelope to ground you to the earth and to discard when the time has come. He says, Puerto Rico is very poor, *chiquita,* but it's a very beautiful country. There is nothing as beautiful as the Caribbean. Then he laughs hard, neighing hee-ha, hee-ha, I just went there, he says. Why do you want me to go back?

They went to look for wood in the street, in the vacant lots adjoining buildings undergoing reconstruction, in the unattended garbage cans at the street corners, those that serve as outdoor stoves, flames leaping orange and a rain of sparks flying about the heads of the drug dealers and the guys keeping watch for the cops, or just warming up their asses, they found some two-by-fours and a couple of splintered chair legs and carried them upstairs to Lulu's apartment, picking up some milk and a pint of rum on the way. The wood crackles in the fireplace Lulu's dug out in the brick wall and decorated with a mantel made of slabs of marble scavenged from the abandoned building's staircase across the street and they bring their coffee and rum chasers on the rug in front of the fire, listening to the hot steam hissing up in the risers, the wind howling outside the windows. Fucking New York winter, Mario says, lying at her feet. You know what, you're right, we should take a trip down there. But not P.R. Maybe Mexico, or Jamaica, hey, what you say?

Lulu thinks of Julian's hand around Salvine's ripe breasts, she sees his white skin with the pale freckles, with the hot/cold touch that turns her into shivers, she sees Julian strung out on her bed, his irises swimming around the white of the eyes with the dead center of the pupils strangely enlarged and vacant. She sees Sherry, whom she's never encountered, giving birth to fat little Henrys gliding out of her cunt, gooey like piglets in the mud.

What's the matter, Lulu, Mario says, cheer up man!

When they make love, it's all smells and juices and textures subtly changing, skin arousing skin, the constant shifting of tastes and flavors, the tongue and the hand forever comparing bulges and rotundities and hollows and cavities. Lulu thinks his skin is spicy, that his sweat tastes like hot curry and he laughs saying she just stereotypes him, you know, big cock, strong smell, virile man. But you're not a hundred percent black, you're mixed blood. Same thing, he says, dark skin, colored people. She says she doesn't care if it's prejudice, he *does* taste like curry and he asks her if she ever tasted real creole curry, and she says no. So she scrapes up some money and he takes her to that Caribbean restaurant lit up with bright-colored neons blurred under corrugated plastic sheets covering the ceiling. There are fake coconut trees with plastic bananas and mangoes all dripping with glitter hanging from them and they drink piña coladas to the tunes of Peter Tosh and Willie Colón, gorging themselves on curried shrimps bathing in a lethal green sauce, it's so hot it makes my skin prickle, Lulu says, yelling in his ear over the music, I bet your sweat is really going to taste curried tonight. My sperm too, he yells back, my sperm gets so hot after I eat that food it burns holes through the girls' throats when they swallow it.

Julian never came to pick her up or to meet her at the Blue Night Lounge, he saw the show once right after they met, but usually he'd show up at her place late at night, or maybe they'd meet for a drink somewhere, but here he is tonight, standing against the bar smoking a cigarette, Lulu suddenly sees him as she and Mystique drop the last of their clothing, jiggling the tufts of ostrich plumes on their nipples to the cheers of the audience. Lulu wonders if he's been there right from the beginning of the show, and as she bends over to salute the audience she waves her fingers at him to acknowledge his presence.

He appears at the dressing-room door, long silent black silhouette. Mystique sees him first and says hi. She's just peeled the little white tufts off her breasts but she's used to having people walk into the room while she dresses or undresses and it doesn't make any difference to her, she could be totally naked it wouldn't make any difference. Lulu is surprised. She doesn't know what she thought, that Julian would vanish with the customers trooping out of the club, that he was a hallucination? He just stays there looking at her, his lips curling up. Take your time, he says. I just want to watch you. She slips on a big black turtleneck sweater, moves her fingers through her short hair, rearranging it. She goes to him, says she's expecting somebody. Who, he asks, sarcastic. Old Saccharine-Daddy Henry?

No. Fuck you.

I didn't know you had another lover.

She says he doesn't know that much about her, and what about Salvine anyway.

What about Salvine?

I know you're lovers. You didn't even tell me.

How do you know that?

Listen. I can tell.

You're paranoid.

And what if she told me.

I don't believe it.

He pushes some accessories aside and sits down on a chair, taking a sip from Mystique's beer can on the makeup table. Lulu never thought she could desire two men at the same time. Henry doesn't count. She doesn't desire Henry so much as . . . Listen, Julian says, you look like a little girl who doesn't know what she wants. Relax. It's going to be interesting. You don't mind if I stick around, do you, an old friend like me? She hates his guts. That's what he's looking for. He's settling on the chair, crossing his legs, lighting a cigarette from Mystique, who's obviously enjoying the situation, taking her sweet time pulling up her leggings and her leg-warmers, while Andrée and Sirouelle split discreetly, throwing their gym bags over their shoulders.

Mystique is making small talk, showing Julian her blue kohl crayons, offering to let him try one, he's smearing the dark blue cosmetic along the inside of his eyelashes, pleased with the result, dabbing a little grey eyeshadow here and there on his eyelids when Mario shows up.

All right man, he says, pointing to Julian's made-up eyes in the mirror. I like it.

Mario is hot fire spreading through the dry underbrush, his energy runs jagged, Julian is cool, burning inside but outwardly detached. He watches Mario throw a fast commentary on the club and what happened to him during the day. Lulu wishes she was somewhere else, or that she was not acquainted with either of them and that any minute now they would leave and she would walk home with Mystique, stopping on the way maybe for a nightcap, but none of them is leaving, and certainly not Julian who now talks about playing poker and Mario says, all right, all right, hitting his thigh with the flat of his hand which seems ludicrous to Lulu until she can't stand it anymore and gets ready to go. Julian gets up and holds her in his arms, kisses moist on the lips, says good-bye, my lovely, his eyes twinkling suggestively and Lulu wants to smack him right in the mouth, but she just pushes him aside, calls, are you coming Mario, walks out in fast strides followed by Mario who asks her, hey, what's the matter, Lulu? She doesn't answer, she just kicks an old beer can in front of her in the street again and again. Stop it, he says. STOP IT. Then he asks, who's that guy Julian? She says, who cares, and he says, you're the one who's doing this big fuss, now I want to know what's wrong. Oh God, she says, holding her face in her gloved hands. I just want to be left alone! And he says, you're really screwy you know.

They got married early one winter day

Mystique is getting married at City Hall, to a Brazilian musician she vaguely knows so that he can get his green card, his name's Fabio. The witnesses are Lulu and a waiter who works at the same restaurant as Fabio. Wanting a respectable ceremony Mystique is wearing her best dress, of lime green wool, under her winter coat, and Fabio is in a suit borrowed from his boss, an off-white affair with bell-bottom legs, circa 1965, looking rather odd in combination with his short army jacket. Fabio's witness, whose name is Ali, is taking Polaroids of them signing the records, but Mystique demands the photos, all of them, and makes him swear never to tell anybody about the wedding, do you hear me, not a soul, which, she realized later, was against the whole purpose of it, but she couldn't care less. Lulu, who has a meeting with an entertainment agent, is in a hurry to get to her appointment and leaves them on the steps of City Hall.

Ali excuses himself promptly afterwards, he has to go back to bed, having gotten up especially for the wedding after only three hours' sleep.

Fabio is shivering in his slight bomber jacket. He looks pale and drawn. He probably didn't have much sleep either. Come on, he says to Mystique with his funny accent, I treat you for breakfast. They find a greasy coffee shop a block down from City Hall, already deserted by the early morning downtown workers, and sit in a booth at the very back, near the bathroom door. It smells of deep-fried doughnuts, of weak American coffee and pine-scented detergent, probably kept with the mop next to the restroom. This is as close as New York gets to America, Mystique tells Fabio, who has no idea what she is talking about.

You sure it's okay not to live together he asks for the hundredth time. Tell me again about the color of your sheets and what you eat for breakfast.

See for yourself, she says, pointing to the oval plate being set in front of her, with a heap of hash browns, three burnt-up strips of bacon and a couple of livid eggs on triangles of anemic and soggy white bread.

He shakes his head. You eat that everyday? Incredulous.

No, she says, if I did chances are I wouldn't have made it so far.

He smiles. He has a very sexy smile in a dark flawless skin and saucer brown eyes, and Mystique remembers she's dreamed about him the night before, his eyes were deep into hers, his smile hovering around her, he didn't touch her but they made love with their eyes, and then she woke up and the first thing she thought was, you're out of your mind. This is the man you're going to marry today. You'd better keep your feelings in check. Besides, he is gay.

She puts her hand over his. It's too bad you're gay. What a pity for women.

I never said I didn't like women, he says.

They look at each other knowingly.

You're not eating?

No. It's too early for me.

He's waiting for her to finish, getting fidgety.

As they get up to pay he passes an arm around her shoulders.

Are you trying to show me you like women?

No, I just wanted to say thank you.

For what? Oh, that. You're welcome. Any time. I just hope your check is good.

It's a few months later. They're waiting in the immigration offices for their interview. A Chinese kid sleeps, head on his arm, leaning against the yellow shabby wall, his glossy hair long on his neck, straight bangs, open shirt, unbuttoned cuffs. An immigrant.

Six-hour wait on the soiled green carpets of the Federal Plaza in the buzz of old-fashioned fans, high on their stems. Asian, black, Slavic faces, tongues with uncertain English, stupor in the eyes from so much wait, eyes deep, deep in their sockets. Numbers called by an invisible voice. Crossed legs that shift from side to side, sleeping Guadeloupean kids, their springy hair woven tight on their skulls. Caribbean French, peppered with English, jumping in the mouths of young and flowered Martiniquaises. The stern voice of a white female immigration officer sharply calling from a door ajar, a glimpse of endless greyish landscape offices, smelling of dust, fingers still sticky with fingerprint ink.

American dreams curtailed in immigration rituals, hushed by third-class lawyers.

I am so scared, Fabio says. What did you say your favorite love position was?

I told you I don't have one. It depends with whom. Or my mood.

But with me, of course. Me, your husband.

All right. Let me think. She looks him in the eyes, her gaze travels down his chest to his crotch, remains there pensive.

I like to do it on the side with you behind me, holding my breasts. I only come that way.

But the officer barely looks at them, just smiles paternally when Mystique, looking demure in a mid-length brown wig, bashfully confesses she is pregnant and is going to meet Fabio's family in São Paulo. The officer actually seems relieved. Fabio walks out with a stamped paper allowing him to travel in and out of the country, his green card pending.

You know what, Mystique tells Lulu on the phone, Fabio just left for California and I don't even have his address there. No, he's not coming back. I don't even have my husband's address can you believe this! What's going to happen to me and the baby? What, Lulu asks. What baby? What are you talking about? Never mind, Mystique says, hanging up.

A pink umbrella in the winter rain

You don't see them. They just go. Their bodies removed. Their memories hushed. You hear of someone, you may even have met her, a friend of your sister's, thirty years old, and all of a sudden, gone. You hear about the genes, bad family history. They are doomed. Marked by the sign. Ill-fated. You hear of heroic fights. Years of pain, never a public complaint. You hear about a new batch of fresh victims every day. Throwing up alone in anonymous aseptic hospital toilets. Hair falling by the handful. Ominous scarfs covering heads down to the eyebrows. A courageous smile on pale, drawn skin. Vital organs removed one after the other, bodies gutted from within, soon a shell to discard. Women wake up on the operating table, their wombs gaping, not with a child squirming to their breast but with the words MALIGNANT TUMOR hung over their heads. It's a bright winter day, but in the hospital all you see is the grey-white of the walls and of the curtains, your pain dulled by the drugs. You can't tell if it's morning or afternoon, you are delirious and believe you might die but it leaves you cold. You think of paintings you did, never finished. You see the red of a woman's blouse. You had worked on this red for days. It was just a shade darker than the background around it, but from a distance emerged a bust clad in something that evoked taffeta. There was a mass of black around the face, figuring the hair. The eyes were very dark, too, burning like fire. There was only this face and the shoulders that escaped the thick brush strokes nervously covering the rest of the canvas. You hung on to this red spot, such a contrast with the ivory-white color of the skin above it. The face is haunting you. You wonder if it is your death you had painted then.

Mystique is sobbing at the door, she is going to die, I know she is going to die, but they won't tell me. They pretend things will be okay. They are liars, fucking liars. She kicks a brown paper bag full of garbage. Two crushed cans of Diet Coke and Miller Lite go rolling down the kitchen floor. Lulu, her chin in her hand, stares at her. Chemotherapy is a dirty word. It gives everybody goosebumps. It's the sound of Death pulling the alarm.

Calm down.

I won't. It's my mother, don't you understand. My flesh, my blood.

I know.

That means I am marked too.

Bullshit.

Yeah. Haven't you ever heard of heredity. He-re-di-ty?

You want a joint?

No.

Lulu hums a tune, very gently. It could be a lullaby from another country, maybe an Arabic melody. It is dawn and peace has finally descended upon the city. For a brief moment, before the garbage trucks start grinding down the streets. We could be lovers, thinks Mystique. This gentleness belongs to lovers. She grunts. *Hushhh* . . . Lulu, sitting next to her on the couch, is stroking her hair.

The rain falls like teardrops from the sky . . . Mystique sings on her way to the coffee shop, the melody sticks to her like old chewing gum to a rubber sole. A copy of *People,* flying in the wind, slides across the sidewalk and lands at her feet. The front page top right corner is ripped and clamors in cryptic caps:

AMERICA
SENDS A
MESS

She picks it up and reads on. Would you invite this man to dinner (under a picture of Boy George), next to one of Ronald Reagan with the caption: Is he too tough? Are we too soft? She stops for a moment, pondering the question.

In the coffee shop the man sitting across the table from her, in black shirt and khaki pants, is chewing a toothpick with an air of furious concentration. His soft grey-brown eyes seem lost in some internal struggle. He makes his felt-tip pen flutter a couple of times between two fingers, pores over his notebook for a minute, then again wags the pen about, ostensibly looking for inspiration. The fluttering of the pen is so distracting she can't even concentrate on the processed prose of *People* so she gazes instead at two flies facing each other at the edge of the table, delicately rubbing their hind legs in a tireless ballet.

The man she picked up at a party two nights before did not seem inclined to soul-searching, unlike this one, he had blue eyes, round shoulders, good pecs, tight round ass, strong hands holding her the right way but he was performing too well, too many workouts maybe, tennis, jogging around the track, timing his laps, measuring his progress on the Nautilus, he was pumping her like an inflatable raft, his breathing coming in and out, in and out perfectly balanced, his lungs filling up, correct breathing, nothing to complain about, but she, in spite of her dance training, suffocated under his hammering body, couldn't keep the tempo, her thighs kept sliding down his waist, her heart beat way too hard, couldn't catch her breath, she was getting drier by the second, her sensations acutely focused on that one place: the cramp spreading across her right hip, but she held on until he collapsed on her saying, oh boy, that was great, how was it for you?

She imagines the man in khaki pressing her against his lean body, his hands fluttering gently in all the right places without being told. He seems to be a soulful type. Maybe his lips would close her wounds. But he gets up and steps out as an explosion of rain spills from the sky turning white to black in a matter of seconds, hammers hard on the pavement, then subsides, turning the snow into muddy slush in the gutters.

Winter rain. Pink umbrella. Water slushing under car wheels. My breasts are getting soft. Ripe grapes. No. Ripe avocados. Mother your face is wrinkled. There is nothing you can do about it. Is that it, are you going to go now? I look for you, hundreds of your faces spanning forty years of our life and all of them eluding me. Are you gone already? Are we both gone? You the tall blond woman with the gingery perfume and the crisp leather gloves, and me, your little mouse of a daughter smooching your lapels with her sticky mouth, but you didn't mind, you whispered sweet secrets in her ear. Your fate can't be sealed. You are alive in my very bones. Black umbrella. Double umbrella. A gadget. With THE NEW YORK TIMES written in large block letters, red on white. I hate endings. There is no happy end. I wind back the film, reread the book, from the middle up. Erase and start all over again. There is that spot, under the eyes. Skin getting loose, slightly sunken if I didn't sleep enough. Now withered. Too thin. Like tissue paper. Crisscrossing fine lines that need daily and nightly nourishing from an expensive cream with collagen, vitamin E and betacaroten. And then they sneak back. They sneaked back on you too. But that is to be expected. Hair turning grey, youth to wisdom. Death a passage from the material world to the spiritual. Or so you told me. But the black war ravaging your entrails is of another order.

It's getting colder and colder at the Blue Night Lounge. There's definitely something wrong with the heating system. The back of the stage is arctic, you wouldn't be surprised to see stalactites hanging over the makeup table. Lulu can't believe this has become a job, to which she shows up four times a week, and where she picks up her check every Friday night. Andrée and Sirouelle are on the verge of being fired. They are on probation for loose behavior, for having kissed and fumbled each other in full view of the audience, while wearing their stage costumes after the show. Even Ed supports them completely. He thinks Marty, the boss, is a prude disguised as a lecherous cabaret owner with diamond rings on each pinkie and greasy hair slicked back. It's because he likes women too much, Mystique says, sarcastic, he can't stand not even having a chance with either one. Ed says he wouldn't think they were his type anyway. Marty called Andrée and Sirouelle fucking dykes and they marched out. There was a reconciliation the next day and they agreed to keep their relationship to themselves, as he put it, after he apologized for his vulgarity and foul temper. But everybody expects a blowup because it's not their style to clam up and pretend everything is hunky-dory.

Lulu tells Mystique she's getting bored, that the atmosphere at the club has distinctly soured since she started in the summer. Mystique says she agrees, but it's not a bad job all the same, that Lulu and her and Andrée and Sirouelle and Ed and even the queens from the drag show are a nice bunch of people, and it's better to work here than in an office. What else would we do? Go-go girls on Forty-second Street? Lulu says they're go-go girls too, although a step up, and Marty's a sleazeball and she's beginning to have had it with the way he pats her butt every time he runs into her backstage, which kind of happens every night lately. Mystique says to tell Marty to fuck off, and that he's a jerk, but he's not altogether a bad guy. Lulu asks her, what about your feminist stance. Mystique turns her eyes away, blowing a spiral of blue smoke that congeals in the polar air, pulling her mouth to one side with the tip of her tongue, then drops with her husky voice, there're economic necessities.

Mystique is loyal. She's been on the job for three years, the longest ever, and she depends on it. She's working on other areas of her life, she doesn't want to worry about subsistence. She says at my age, you don't want to be jumping from job to job on a whim and reinventing your life every other week. You have other business to attend to. She doesn't say what. What it means is that she is dead opposed to a general strike in support of Andrée and Sirouelle's plight, which Lulu would favor for it would relieve them of the freezing cold evenings while allowing them to perform a generous and politically correct act. But anyway Andrée and Sirouelle don't want to hear about it. They don't want to jeopardize everybody's jobs.

Lulu tells Mystique she can't stand kicking her legs up with tassles dangling from her boobs anymore. She's going to Mexico with Mario. But you'll keep the job for me, right, Mystique? Marty tells her he's sorry, but she'll have to take the chance, he's not going to wait for her to come back, he'll have to take someone to replace her at least temporarily. Lulu doesn't want to worry about it. She's got to get out of here.

The deal is to get a used car, drive like hell through the south, cross Mexico all the way to the Yucatán, spend some time there, sell the car and fly back to New York. The peso is so cheap right now they think they can hang in there for a month or two, roast in the subtropical sun while you guys bundle up to your ears and grow green skin in the dark, come back in the spring. Sounds good, don't you think? Sounds good to me!

All they see is cheapo eleven-dollars-a-night motels with the tv anchored to the ceiling and a shot of Magic Fingers before sleeping, and the long ribbon of highway on a background of country music, until they hit the Rio Grande, and then, *hombre,* it's all cacti and red dust flying high at their wheels and Mario starts relaxing. *Mexico, hombre! Mexico!*

Lulu's diary in Mexico:

Yesterday we took the leap into the heat, the dust, through the frenetic, colorful, begging Mexican border. We stayed two hours at the immigration offices, waiting for our passports to be stamped, watching the cockroaches die.

What a scream, this first hotel: a few dirty cubbyholes with two-inch-long scared cockroaches crawling on the floor around a patio, a hole in the mud floor for the toilet and another hole for the shower. In the morning I drank Pepsi for breakfast because I was scared to get sick from the water. Mario made fun of me, he said the coffee was delicious, he could see little amoebas floating in it. But I'm going to look for pills to purify the water.

SUNDAY, ZIHUATANEJO

We've driven straight down to the ocean, Mario couldn't wait to see it. He's never been to the Pacific Coast. He got his Levi's stolen on the beach with his watch in it, but the hotel is real nice, with palm trees and other tropical plants on the patio. Mario picked a guanabana from one of the trees outside our bedroom and we ate it. It's a green spiky fruit, bigger than a mango, with a heavy, white flesh that tastes a little like lychee.

We drink squeezed lime juice and mango *con leche* and coconut milk straight from the nuts (they drill a hole through them) and we make love in the afternoon in our mildewed bedroom under the fan.

Sitting at her kitchen table Mystique is writing to Lulu on one of these ridiculously expensive handmade papers, of a delicate ivory tone, the kind made with real pressed wood through which you can see twigs flattened between the layers of pulp. It's so thick it almost absorbs the ink like a blotter. She writes,

> Dear Lulu,
>   I miss you, New York is a fucking icebox, Marty's still a sleazeball and I haven't had a man in two weeks.

. . .

and stops to look at the results, which rather pleases her. Fattish letters, straight purple line (she loves purple ink and writes with a gold-tip fountain pen), slanting upwards. She once read in a graphology manual it was a sign of optimism. She flatters herself on her positive outlook on life. *Une imbécile heureuse,* says Lulu. A happy idiot. Even the reality of death didn't deter her optimism. Until . . . She fights a vision of her mother gripping the side of her bed in an effort to curb the nausea. Mystique's motto is, we have a whole life to live before dying. Optimism is an intellectual choice, then? A cold-blooded, rational choice. Maybe a substitute for despair. Red-hot optimism like a lid on white wan despair.

My mother is back home she goes to the hospital for the chemo shots. The dosage is heavy and it makes her very sick. I'm not sure she realizes . . . She says, a woman can live without a uterus. I didn't need it any more . . . She started drinking again. I found her asleep with a half-empty quart of whiskey in front of her on her kitchen table the other day. It scares me Lulu. I don't know what to do.

Three clocks, made from LPs spray-painted pink and mauve, their arms of clear plastic, show three different times next to her on the wall. Only one of them tells the correct time. The trick is to know which one is right. Mystique does, of course, only sometimes she has a moment of hesitation.

When she left New York, Lulu was wearing a velvet turban out of which emerged a few strands of blond hair. She had put together a vague twenties look with a long narrow woollen dress, laced suede boots and a fur-collared coat. Mystique watched her climb aboard the beat up Mercury Mario had dished up from a questionable source on East Sixth Street, then waved her fingers to them as the car started off. The pin, Mystique yelled, your pin fell off, and she rummaged in the gutter, pulling out a small pin made of a silver hand grasping a feather that had slipped out of Lulu's turban. Mystique had given it to her as a bon voyage gift. It's a good-luck pin, she said. Hang onto it. In answer

Lulu yanked it through the velvet, pointing to it with a finger as the car turned the corner.

Mystique tries to picture Lulu in Dallas, or L.A., or Mexico City, wherever she is. She pours herself a Scotch and, glass in hand, goes to the mirror to examine her face. She pinches the skin underneath her eyes, in order to check, one more time, that it doesn't spring back as before, that it has, as they say in beauty products ads targeted at—who else?—women over thirty-five (an age still considered by ad agencies as the beginning of the end), anyway, as Revlon & Co. says: that it has lost its elasticity. Feeling mean, she pinches again and the skin holds the nasty fold for an eternity, giving her a taste of the next decade. So you thought you'd be young forever? She turns off the light over the sink, a light that would give circles under the eyes of a twelve-year-old anyway, and pees in the dark. Mom, I won't let you die, she whispers, we'll fight it off together.

TUESDAY

We went skinny dipping last night. There was no moon. The water was warm but the waves were huge and dark and you couldn't see more than a couple of yards away. You could hear the thunder from a distance. I was scared and I stayed near the beach just jumping in the waves. Juan, the Mexican from the hotel, came with us and he was on the make for me, but Mario kept swimming around us. I think Mario has changed since we passed the border. He seems to be more macho. He was very upset that I didn't wear a bathing suit because Juan was with us. He said it looked like I was leading him on. But Mario didn't have his bathing suit on either and it was so good to feel the waves roll over my skin.

Three women
in red

The three women were in red. In red lace. There was a profusion of scarlet lace, crimson velvet dresses, a carmine shawl or cape thrown over the back of a chair. First they were faceless, then Lulu could make out their very white skin and jet-black hair. The room looked like one in those castles she used to visit as a child outside Paris, La Malmaison or Saint-Germain-en-Laye, with Louis XVI armchairs and sofas heavily damasked in deep reds and blues filigreed with faded golds. The furniture was spare and rigidly arranged. On the walls hung huge gold-framed portraits of bewigged ancestors whose rouged lips and high heels seemed to promise equivocal pleasures. A harpsichord played with a strange flat metallic sound, like an out-of-tune pianola. The women sat around a low table, a fire blazing behind them in a high carved-wood fireplace. One of them opened her ring, an oval amethyst heavily set in gold that served as a lid for a small cache, and swallowed a little of the white powder kept in it with the tip of a silver spoon. They each swallowed in turn some of the substance which Lulu knew to be poison, gravely, like faithful receiving the Holy Host. Then they got up and fetched a young girl, her head covered with a black veil. At the very moment Lulu recognized her as her own daughter, she knew the child was condemned. My baby, my little one! she sobbed, throwing herself at her feet, holding her tight. Tears rolled down her cheeks. The girl, who had been standing very straight, suddenly grew dizzy, wavered, and hung onto her. Lulu got up and screamed. No! NO! Not her, not my child. She heard her own scream reverberate down the empty hallways leading out of the room. But already the child had slipped on the rug and one of the women was clutching her chest, and slowly the red lace turned to blood, blood spilling down the inlaid floor, splashing the fireplace mantel, each woman was a large pool of blood, and Lulu's scream froze, absorbed by the thickness of curtains and draperies, while the harpsichord kept grinding its harsh quick tune, as if mocking the scene, louder and louder. Lulu woke up to the sound of the coffee grinder buzzing in the kitchen on the other side of the paper-thin wall of their hotel room, and she covered her face with her hands.

Mexico's sun is glaring and white; its villages, poor and sad. Lulu finds no trace of the Latin *joie de vivre* she expected. She wonders if the sadness is in her, and why. It'll be different in the south and the east, in Oaxaca, in the Yucatán, Mario promises. This is the poorest part of the country. Poignant scenes roll slowly past their car windows. Bare-assed little kids playing with pebbles on the side of the road, running toward the car with their hands outstretched; this beggar without arms and legs, a mere trunk fastened to a piece of wood mounted on wheels pulled by a little boy, positioned at the exit road out of Monterrey. Their second day in Mexico, they were hit by an electric storm that lasted a whole night. At each flash of lightning three-forked cacti lit up in twisted agony for interminable seconds, green and spiky against the sky's ominous gray, then faded into the stormy night. I wish we were traveling by bus, Lulu remarks. We might get to know the people better.

On the way to Guadalajara, Lulu launches into one of her monologues. I grew up thinking I was an orphan, she says. Which I was not, of course, since my father was alive. But the word "orphan" had attractive connotations. A Cinderella without stepmother. An Eliza Doolittle. Except I was never in wait for Prince Charming or Pygmalion. I didn't need another father in my life. The idea of being an orphan was thrilling. I felt hurled out in the world on my own, like a bullet in flames surging through life. I pictured myself with hard edges and a heart of steel. It gave me the chills. Supergirl flying through space, with hair two inches long and a laser in her hand. What's the matter? Do you find that ridiculously naive?

Mario is a good listener, maybe because his prolonged silences serve as voids into which she tosses uncensored bits and pieces of her mind, like fluttering thoughts cast to the wind or diary entries. One day, a few days after they left New York, she said to him, you're like a wall against which I play ball. Thanks, he said, turning his back to her. You don't understand, she'd gone on. It's a rare virtue. You barely interfere, but you are a presence, you are receptive. He'd grumbled, unconvinced. He lets her rant and rave, with enough encouragement here and there to keep her going. Punctuation marks. Mostly nonjudgmental. Although occasionally she can almost feel his flesh ripple and his eyes cloud if she gets off the track too long or ventures upon ground too abstract. The trail of dust suddenly settles around them, leaving a thin pink-beige layer on the car hood. A brand new asphalt road marks the entrance to a small town. They stop for gas and drink orzeta under the cool arcades of the town *zócalo*. The colors are shades of cantaloupe and dusty papaya and the soiled white of the *campesinos* coming back from work, machetes swaying at the hip.

When they start off again the heat is letting up somewhat and the temperature becomes more comfortable even with the windows rolled up against the dust. She tells him about her dream and the women in red take a plunge down the void. The women were lesbians, she adds after a silence. What do you think it means? I don't know, he says finally. That you find women dangerous? Powerful? Desperate? I had another dream about you, she continues. It was taking place in the same room, with the fire in the fireplace. You were alone and you held the ring in your hand. You took the poison too. Nobody made you do it. It was . . . like you were accepting your fate. You died, your face down on a table, without struggle. Was I wearing a wig? he asks. She hits his knee with her fist. You jerk! No. You were like yourself. Except you didn't have your Ray-Bans. What do you think it means? And as he shrugs without venturing an opinion, she says, I think it was the poison of American society, synthesized in the all-purpose white powder. Nice metaphor, huh?

The car breaks down around 8 P.M. on a deserted stretch of the road. It's been heating up all day and they've had to stop every half-hour or so to cool out, refilling the radiator with water stocked in jerry cans. Now bursts of smoke spit out from the front of the hood with an acrid smell of burnt rubber. The leak's gotten worse, Mario says, slamming the door behind him. Lulu stays inside. Mario attacks mechanical problems with an intense passion, only to fall into frustration when he cannot fix them right away. What's the matter, she asks as he comes back to pick up a rag, after furiously rummaging through the trunk. No answer. He's making angry noises behind the hood. She gets out, bends over the guilty radiator. It's probably got a hole, she offers, peering hard in the dark.

Thanks for the diagnosis!

He's trying to direct the beam of the flashlight through the small opening.

Can you hold this please?

What about from below?

He glares at her. Be my guest.

She lies down on the dirt road, her head under the motor block, peers and feels around with one hand. The metal is peeling rust under her fingers, chunks of it are falling on her neck. Then her hand goes right through something, emerging on the other side of the thin metal sheet.

We'd better not fool around with it anymore, she says, pulling out from under. The radiator wall's like paper. All you've got to do is poke a finger at it, and it crumbles.

Let me see. Goddamn it! There's a hole the size of my fist. Fuckin' A! He kicks the side of the car with his boot, in a resigned burst of anger. The strip of metal running along the door falls out. The car is a spacious Mercury sedan with blown shock absorbers. We can sleep in it, Lulu says. Mario groans. *Hijo de puta!* Those *maricones* on Sixth Street! Man, I can't believe it! At least the air-conditioning's pretty good, she observes. Mario looks at her blankly. No more, baby, he says. Not with a busted radiator.

In the huge, rambling Guadalajara market, the tourists are clad in white pleated shirts and wide loose trousers parading around like bleached-out *campesinos*. While Mario is buying a pair of leather sandals, Lulu drifts toward the piles of ripe fruit rising in green, orange and red pyramids in the food section of the *mercado*. The bananas in thick clusters are small with a lemony flavor and she buys a bunch of them, along with butter-ripe avocados to squeeze into fresh *bolillo* breads, like Mario told her he used to do in P.R. Indian women with purple cheeks and slit-eyed babies strapped across their backs sell green oranges full of pits and tamales wrapped in banana leaves, while they keep busy sculpting mangoes in the shape of flowers they carefully arrange in wicker baskets. They are sitting crosslegged on richly woven maroon pieces of cloth, the very kind that makes some tourists salivate and prompts them to offer their Timex or Instamatic in exchange, letting the fabric go to the moths at the bottom of a trunk when they bring it back home.

The hotel is near the market, off a small square shaded by magnolia trees. Two floors of rooms overlook a tiled patio open to the sky. Potted palms sway outside the doors amid worn-out bamboo furniture. Lulu and Mario sit on a sofa and spread their food in front of them on a small table. How long do you figure we're going to have to stay here? Lulu asks, tarting up her avocado sandwich with a dash of lime juice. Why, don't you like it? It's okay, she says. As soon as the car's ready, we go. Or as long as we feel like it. Sounds good to you? he asks cheerfully, hugging her in a tight embrace. I don't know, she says, moving her shoulders to push his arm away.

They lie on the sunken mattress with the top sheet pulled out. His skin is amber and turns a warm caramel in the sun. She keeps hers creamy white with heavy doses of sunscreen and a wide-brimmed straw hat. The contrast between their skin color turns them on and she licks the inside of his arm from his palm to his armpit, listening to his breathing quickening. She goes down his chest, following the thin line of hair between his pecs with the tip of her tongue, running it to his bush of black curls and around his cock. Teasing. Circling it, then going down a leg, working around his foot and under it till his groan comes out helpless. Then she gets up to take a shower. Shit! he complains, lying crucifix-like in the middle of the bed, his penis a purple column of desire. What do you do to a man. Lulu! Come back, man. Finish what you started! Her cool laugh pearling through the patter of drops against the bathroom tiles gives him goosebumps.

She was standing in a moonlike landscape. She climbed on a soft dirt slope and found herself surrounded by rows of bystanders massed along a road. All the eyes were turned in the same direction. She waited with the others. A drumlike rumble first announced that whatever they were waiting for was coming. She pulled herself on tiptoes and stretched her neck. The rumble turned into a clatter of thousands of feet. A parade appeared at the far bend of the road, hundreds and hundreds of people, with dogs, cats, even farm animals, a slow exodus. The movement in the crowd, the running up and down, the laughing and shouting, the vivid colors of the clothes, the music emerging here and there, louder as the procession reached her, reminded her of sixties marches she'd seen on documentaries, but without the banners and the slogans. In fact, these people were hardly marching at all, they were flowing in a gigantic mass, a human river fed by groups of onlookers constantly joining and thickening the human tide, now barely contained within the slopes embanking the road. The sun, earlier brilliant and high in the sky, was setting on what had become fields of green wheat rippling under the late afternoon breeze. It was a warm summer day, there was moisture rising from the soil around them, its smell rich and almost greasy, and a chant coming up in waves, dying with a group, picked up by another. Then it happened. The sun, which had grown to a large flat orange disk on the prairie-like horizon, turned black. A cry of horror poured out of thousands of mouths, cascading down the road swarming with marchers as far as the eye could see. People ran out in the fields, tripping over one another. Animals neighing, barking, lurched into the wave of runaways, causing fatal accidents. Parents clutched their children and tried to find an escape from the crowd as if fire had caught in their midst. The black sun grew larger, was filling half the sky. It was dark, almost as if night, but the sky remained blue. Then it turned to red, leaving a jagged circle of fiery orange leaping out around the blackness. Cries of anger, of God have pity on us rose repeatedly. In the panic people got trampled, dying under the rush of a crowd gone berserk. Lulu sat up in a sweat and shielded her eyes against the sun blinding her as she woke up on a bench of the little square where she had fallen asleep. Come on, it's getting hot, she heard Mario's voice above her. It's not good to sleep in the sun. The car's ready. Let's go to the hotel and pack. He pronounced hotel in a funny way, which she told him once she thought was typically nuyorican, but he didn't seem to get what she meant and only commented on her own accent.

In Zihuatanejo they kill time in a hotel room with mildew on the ceiling and cool white and blue tiles on the floor. It is steamy hot. The fan is broken and the only window, overlooking the inside patio, is closed with wooden shutters that won't come unstuck. The name of the hotel is El Zócalo. Time passes, indifferent to them. Lying on his stomach on yet another sunken bed, his dark skin shining over well-drawn muscles, Mario is asleep, one arm hanging from the bed. He's kept his Ray-Bans on, those with the white frame, which he wears to pass incognito, he says. His bare, muscular back has become part of the landscape, along with the caved-in mattresses, the smell of mildew on the sheets, the palms on the patios, the broken tiles. Every hotel the same, with their two naked bodies and the way he likes to suck her breasts when they start making love. She turns over and leans on her elbow to light up a roach, and wonders what the fuck she's doing there.

Mexican diaries

MEXICO CITY. SATURDAY

I've got the runs. The *turistas*. The whole night every ten minutes in the bathroom. What a night! I think it's that cactus salad I ate at the market yesterday that was full of cilantro. Letter from Mystique today at the general delivery. Her mother's not responding to chemo. She's really worried. The coffee here is delicious, almost like in Paris. We spend hours in a café near the *zócalo* drinking *café con leche* and eating *molletes* (toasted bread with butter).

MONDAY

Feeling better today. Went to see our first pyramids at Teotihuacán. We drove with an American couple we met at the American Express office in Mexico City. The site is beautiful, surrounded by a circle of green and blue mountains. The best one is the Pyramid of the Sun. It is renovated on one side, the other three are partially collapsed and overgrown with grass, but the proportions are beautiful. The problem was to walk up there. It's very steep and the steps are narrower than the length of a foot, and I had vertigo after a while, especially when Mario started telling us that if you miss a step, there is nothing you can hang on to, you roll all the way down. I took off my shoes and went on barefoot. The view was great. Too bad there were all these tourists up there with their cameras. But that's exactly what we are.

Mario is getting on my nerves. He doesn't like me to get too friendly with the Americans and the French we meet. He says it's because he doesn't want to hang out with the *gringos,* but I think he's jealous. He's really turning macho.

SATURDAY

We had our photos taken on the Parque de Alameda, near Bellas Artes. What a scream! There are all these old photographers with antique cameras shooting families of Indians decked out in their best clothes, and I thought it would be nice to have our picture taken as a souvenir from Mexico. So we found this little toothless guy operating a green box on a tripod. We sat on two chairs, with a grey fabric hung behind us as backdrop. The old man put his hand through a canvas hose coming out of the box and shook up something inside. With his other hand he pulled on a string. The little bird had to come out several times because Mario kept making faces. Finally the photographer showed us the negatives, printed on paper (!), and immediately plunged them into a tub of water or acid. Then he set the negative on a piece of wood that sprang up in front of the lens, and he re-photographed the negative, to get the negative's negative, which is to say the photo of Mario looking like a *guerrillero* and me like a prisoner escaped from a concentration camp. *Et voilà!* Guaranteed WWII look.

THURSDAY

Still in Mexico City. We went to the zoo and then we had a

horrible fight that lasted until one o' clock in the morning. We were so starved we left the hotel to get some food at our favorite café, Super Leche, where we stayed until it closed with a few hookers taking a break before their last shift.

PUEBLA. SUNDAY

The car broke down again today right after we arrived in Puebla. Lucky it wasn't on the road. This time it's really serious. Something the matter with the gearshift. We spent the whole afternoon looking for a garage that could take care of it. Finally we found this guy who said he was going to try to fix it, but if he has to order a part from Mexico City or the States . . . forget it!

OAXACA. MONDAY

It's too boring to wait in Puebla for the car, there isn't that much to do there, so last night we just went to the station to see if there were trains going anywhere. There was one for Oaxaca scheduled on the bulletin board to leave at a quarter to eleven and we decided to take it.

All these people in the station. People bundled up on the benches, kids sitting on the floor, kids begging at the doors. People sleeping outside, under the arcades, wrapped up in a blanket. There is this French guy sitting next to us on a bench in the waiting room, he looks a little like Raphael, his hair, or rather his lack of hair, and these big blue eyes. He is reading Robbe-Grillet. He loves the waiting room. He says it's great. It's terrifying. What am I doing here. What are my eyes doing here, in this place I don't understand and will never understand. I tell him there are kids sleeping under the bench. But he keeps reading without showing any emotion. Mario says it's like that in Puerto Rico. I don't belong here. I hate these people who see me just like a tourist with pesos. Even their urge toward us I don't understand. I don't dare look at them, their shawls, their kids, their fatigue. I don't know what I would say to them, what I feel. Maybe pity.

I bought a beautiful sarape in the market woven in dark red

and brown. We went to see the Monte Alban ruins. Less impressive but more peaceful than Teotihuacán. A peasant boy hidden in the bushes called as we wandered away and offered us little clay statues he said he'd found in the country. Apparently you can still find authentic Mayan figurines in the ruins so we bought three (they were the same price as the copies they sell in town), hoping there might be a chance they were genuine . . .

MÉRIDA. WEDNESDAY

We got the car back. We went to Veracruz, Palenque, Campeche. We fight every day. Mario complains that I don't make any progress in Spanish (but we always speak English together, how can I?) and that I prefer to hang out with other travelers. We fight about picking up hitchhikers, about what he calls "my continual flirting with men," about his lack of interest in the culture, about his silences and our mutual boredom. Maybe we're not good travelers.

I hitchhiked to Chichén Itzá on my own, Mario refused to go see one more pyramid. I climbed on all fours I was so scared of the height and I saw the most beautiful sunset of my life from the the top of the pyramid: it's hard to describe (I took photos of it), there were two huge cones of yellow light streaming out of a purple cloud in the middle. Eerie.

ISLA MUJERES. MAY 15

This is paradise island. Sand white and fine like icing sugar, jade-green sea, coconut trees gracefully bent against the pure sky. Multicolored fish caroming around in the transparent water when you go snorkeling. But it's no paradise for me. I think

What are you doing? Mario says. Again writing in your diary! That's all you like about traveling, writing about it? Can't you just enjoy it, goddamn it! Just relax, enjoy.

They found this room by the beach for a few pesos, rented by a fat and obnoxious Frenchwoman who says she knows "all the Americas." Brazil is the best, she says. But Brasilia? The work of a madman. There is only Rio.

Why don't you go to the beach? The water is *deliciosa*.

Lulu says, Mario, I think I'm pregnant.

He doesn't take it too well. His tan turns grey. He asks are you sure, how can you be sure? several times. He pulls out a little brown paper bag from his pocket and starts rolling a joint, takes a couple of long puffs without offering her any. He nods. He says, man, it's fucked up, what are we going to do? What are we going to do? Hey, it's not so tragic, she says. New York City is full of abortion clinics. He says, man, my baby!

Your baby?

What? It's not mine?

Lulu gets up to take a puff from the joint. She says she didn't mean that. Just that there's no baby right now. She's pregnant, that's all. An accident. An unfortunate lapse. He's got this damn possessive attitude. He tells her they're stuck here. They don't have the dough to fly back. He's going to have to sell the car.

I can't wait, Mario. I'll ask Henry to wire me some money.

Who's Henry?

A friend. A rich friend.

Now Mario starts raising hell. Lulu suggests they go to the beach. Mario gets back on the subject in front of a plate of *ceviche de concha* at a little restaurant set up in the shade of a palm roof a couple of yards from the sea. He wants to know who Henry is. Lulu says he's an old friend, a friend of her family. He's always helped when she was in trouble. Mario seems to calm down. They go swimming and lie down dripping under a coconut tree. Mario begs her to wait for him in New York, not to do anything in a huff. We could get married, he says finally, stroking her hair and smiling tenderly. Lulu's horrified. A little *niño,* he says. That would be nice. Chocolate brown. Racially mixed kids are beautiful. Lulu pulls back, sits up. I don't want to talk about this, she says.

But Lulu, think about it. We could do it. Man, it would be beautiful. A little baby. My mother would love it.

The zeitgeist

Arriving in New York is like penetrating a different time zone. The experience is of a different order than cultural shock. It's like taking a trip in a time machine. People look like they came out of a sci-fi cartoon strip. Bizarre haircuts and attitudes, the pitch of their voices, their innuendos, even the shape of their bodies seems unnatural, slightly mutant. Angular knees, overdeveloped cheek-bones, clawlike fingernails, the hair going out in patches, the skin abnormally white. Perhaps it's some disease, some latent form of AIDS, or a more concentrated absorption of chemicals in foods and in the air, the high level of carbon monoxide. After a while you realize that the disease is in the mind. Which you should have known in the first place, for hadn't you been told that all disease springs from the mind? One of its symptoms is the feeling of being permanently onstage and having to perform well at all times. Even nonactors feel compelled to compete as fiercely as if a Broadway career was at stake. You have to know how to play with signs. A lot of it has to do with your looks: fifties nihilistic crossed with early sixties nerd, a touch of punk, a sea of black. A strident haircut. A drop-dead expression on a livid face. Everybody priding themselves on not being normal, but, coming from Europe, you have no idea what American normal can possibly mean. Look for the perfect hairdresser and get the perfect cut. Start again a month later. Be obsessed with your looks. A field in which your creativity and sense of the *zeitgeist* (it takes awhile to understand what it means, and even longer to venture to use the word) are constantly tested. New York is no different than Paris, or Montreal, or Amsterdam, or L.A., but instead of offering well-established codes, New York demands that you be ahead of constantly changing ones.

A container was discovered in southern California with remnants of 16,500 little bodies in rigor mortis. They were dead foetuses, shipped from various abortion clinics and hospitals to a "laboratory" for "experiments," and were on their way to storage. Some workers found them by accident, as they were carrying the container, and the contents spilled on the ground. They said they saw "dismembered bodies," "hands, torn right off." According to the *Daily News,* they cried and vomited at the sight. "Grown men weeping and vomiting," were the terms used by the article. The workers said they counted the fingers and looked at "legs with little kneecaps torn off the body." They said they looked for the head, and realized "there ain't no head."

Lulu stares at the clipping that she carefully cut from the *News* with her nail scissors. It rests neatly on her kitchen table, with the columnist's photo smiling benignly at her from the left-hand corner. It speaks of burial without religious ceremony as if that was the point. She doesn't feel shame. Only awe that the foetuses were that developed. How old must they have been for anyone to be able to count fingers? Four months, six months? How can anyone carry a child so long and still go ahead with an abortion? She imagines the agony of waiting so long. She read about that woman who, wide awake during her abortion, asked to look, to see what it was that was coming out of her. In Lulu's case it would look like menstrual fluid, but when it's already been five months, more than halfway there, then what? And does that make a difference, anyway? A century ago they didn't believe foetuses had a soul before the fourth or the sixth month. But then, at one point, they didn't believe that women had a soul either. Or Negroes, for that matter. The thing about life is that it doesn't spring out all completed like Athena out of Zeus' head, it unfurls gradually. Even death is not so clear-cut.

I think you're sick to cut these clippings and keep them, says Mystique when she sees that Lulu stacks them in a folder locked in a filing cabinet. What for? Jesus. I don't believe this. It's fucking masochistic. Lulu says that it's not, she's just collecting evidence. Mystique asks, evidence of what? Lulu says she doesn't know. And anyway maybe they're right. Maybe it is a crime. Maybe it is a holocaust.

Oh Christ! Is that what you feel like, a criminal?

No.

Women my age fought for years to get free abortion instead of using coathangers or knitting needles and hemorrhaging in dirty kitchens. And you're having states of mind about it.

I am entitled to my states of mind.

Mystique's eyes soften. Sometimes she turns motherly with Lulu. At least motherly the way Lulu likes to think of it, loving, reassuring, nurturing, understanding.

You're right, she says. At least as far as your states of mind are concerned.

Lulu says she won't survive New York, its breathless vitality. It's like being on coke twenty-four hours a day. It's like spending your life denying death.

Isn't all life a form of denial of death?

Maybe. Oh shit, I don't know. But I don't think I can live up to my own expectations. This city forces you to have high expectations. People keep saying, don't put so much pressure on yourself. But that's a way of life here.

I believe that people who end up in New York are people who

have high expectations about themselves to begin with. You come here to measure yourself. Whatever.

Whatever. I can't measure myself. I go back and forth in time and space and in circles. Sometimes I blimp out. Sometimes I levitate. Sometimes I expand around the universe. It's a joke. We're all blinking fireflies and we want to measure ourselves.

Shhh, Mystique says. You're speaking against the myth. Don't let anyone hear you.

Red moon

It is 3 A.M. Pouring rain like a tidal wave crashing against the windows. Lulu's apartment pitches heavily in the roaring storm. Manhattan is a ship-island tossed about the swollen seas swept by the winds. All the lights are off except the lightning discharging at an incredible speed zipping down the electric lines, through her belly, through her entrails swollen with child, the fullness of her uterus, of her breasts tender, alive. Sitting cross-legged in the middle of the mattress she clutches her body, the tide of the storm rising and exploding, rising and exploding with the nausea in her throat.

The rain lashes against the windows covered with steam.

There is no story. Only cycles repeating themselves ad infinitum. No beginning no end just voices clashing. Too many voices too many voices. The soft one the violent one. A knife through the liver it takes and then you gasp. The little girl in the street with her Mickey Mouse from Disney World. When you said we met in Paris at Les Deux Magots in 1933, I thought, for a brief moment, that I remembered it. I ache for all these other lives. Maybe I can live them if I repaint my floor cerulean blue and change my wardrobe.

I miss the ocher that melts that explodes, the gorgeous red, the scarlet of damask velvets, the amaranth of the satin. In your sweet-tasting armpits the tongue runs, the nostril sniffs, gorges itself. A Latin guitar, a sentimental Castilian voice singing *corazón* and *amor* in the sweet heat of *la noche de Nueva York*.

But there is no nostalgia in New York. The past dies every day. Murdered, demolished, burned, abandoned.

Outside the window, the olive-green hills of Provence, covered with ripening vines. I see her, my mother, during the war, walking down the steps of a terrace in a white linen dress with a wide collar billowing in the wind, waving to the young man with the black curly hair, David, the man from the snapshot I found in the dresser.

Inside my belly something is blubbering, pushing its way out. A foreign organism, a mussel, an amphibian creature has attached itself to my uterus by accident, determined to grow there. And I am going to deliver you to the abortionist. *Faiseuse d'anges,* they used to say. Angel makers. Oh, probably a very respectable doctor. And why do I hope it will be a woman? Accomplices to murder. Swift soft gestures. A woman's quarter's ritual. The botched-up jobs in the backroom, the failures, the miscarriages *entre nous*. To spare the men, that they only attend the glorious birth, the successful act, ten toes, no webbed foot, two eyes, one nose, the birth cry, the first breathing, everything working. But not the shameful dripping, the scraping and the curetting, the nozzles that push their way, threatening, between the teeth of the speculum. You sound like a conservative bigot, the doctor says. But *we* are the murderers. Come on, admit that the feminists made a mistake about abortion. His blond hair, his cool, his white blouse. He asks me, why isn't your boyfriend with you? But how dare he, how dare he ask me these insidious questions.

Why do you think you find yourself pregnant? What do you think it means, psychoanalytically?

In the village all the stores were closed until four. From noon till four. Who would be crazy enough to go work in that heat, the sun beating hard. The bushes dry as tinder. A match casually thrown would set fire to the whole mountain in minutes.

The dry Mediterranean heat of the summertime. The sun spilling without a chance of escape. The clear and hard heat that pounces down on the ocher, arid soil, the bluish-green of the pine land, the khaki-green of the olive grove. The short and thick vine that clings to the hillside. The *maquis*. They walked together, first down toward the vineyards, then up the hill across from the village, holding hands.

From the depth of her belly, an unavowable desire, disturbing, downright at odds with the survival instinct. The two of them at war. Not a desire. A blind push. An irresponsible, animal swelling. Unrelenting like the sun. That you have to do violence to yourself to thwart. A thrust of nature which doesn't mean a thing. Amoral. Like the sun pouring down, unconscious of its burn, bringing life and death at the same time.

Against which you fight back. Or else you catch the wind, the boat listing, sails skimming the water line. But sometimes sailing against the waves. The nausea rises like waves too. She gags on her toothbrush. Her intestines are running wild. How can she make a decision when the body is out of control, does its little personal gig without asking for her permission? Joins forces with nature? Makes her puke in the toilets and on the side of the roads just like she did when she was a little girl, hanging out the front window of the old Peugeot her father drove on the Provence back roads?

A uterine tide. No, earthly. No, aquatic. You build a jetty. It breaks down. Bang. The water rams through it, overflows it. Covers everything up. Sweeps up the land. The mechanism is set in motion. And to stop it you have tricks. Woman is smart enough for that. You try to outwit nature. But there is resistance in your head. You've got to take that into account. It's the part of the belly which lives in the head. Which takes nature's side. Traitor. You are head and body all at once and it tears you apart.

She holds the quartz crystal in her hand. Octagonal cut. There are planes that are more roughly cut, that throw rainbows in the sun. She turns it around between her fingers. Her eyes plunge through its layers. It's like clear water caught frozen. The transparency is perfect, here polished, there frosted. The inside bristles with iridescent crystals.

There are waves of guilt that ride up to her lips, her throat, that keep coming back. Children's faces bursting with life.

I'm a little teapot
short and stout
here is my handle
here is my spout
when I get all steamed up
I will shout
just tip me over
and pour me out

She passes a string of kids holding hands singing in the street on their way to the park. They curl their arms as they sing to mimic the handle of a teapot. She's going to smother one of theirs in the egg. It will join the heaps of foetuses the Moral Majority loves to dig out of garbage cans. A kid's embryo who would one day have smiling eyes and dimples. Who would one day be a man, my son. Or a woman.

At exactly nine-thirty at the church tower, every evening at dusk, the swallows hover in formation above the vale, circling the village. The sky is pale, greyish-pink. They cheep. They fly across the twilight, their wings spread out, very black. The moon appears at the same time, a piece of gauze floating toward the south. The swallows wheel around, they jabber loudly. They are very busy. They seem to do something extremely specific. It lasts ten minutes. Then they fly away before the night comes down.

They still hadn't come back when the swallows took off. They stopped to eat some *saucisson* sandwiches and red wine before the sun set. The *mistral* was getting strong. They resumed their walk, pushing the bushes out of their path, climbing toward the top of the hill. He was dressed in sportsgear, almost military, with a small backpack on his shoulders. In spite of her smart clothes she had espadrilles on. They walked on briskly in the cool night, in silence.

They were called women of sacrifice. It was a good thing to be. Especially when matched with men of duty. They made a perfect couple. It had an aftertaste of washing machines and frigidity. Close your eyes and grit your teeth. But it was a way to reach paradise or at least the lesser women of sacrifice's jealous admiration. It was something that mattered, that had meaning.

Lulu is looking at herself. She sees a face of the earth. Two shadows running from her nose down to her mouth, stubborn and dark. Something hard coming from the earthy heredity, bitter, responsible, serious. Without the grace which came later, working its way through it, illuminating. The grace of pleasure, seduction.

Myra Schneider keeps appearing in her dreams. In them she is younger than in reality. Her beauty is full-blown and dazzling. She dances in a dress of white muslin with an officer in Navy uniform. She dances in a black silk sheath open down to her waist, slit up to the knees, with a man she meets every night on the marble floor of a grand ballroom. They slowly dance their way toward the high plants framing the entrance to a small sitting room. Behind the plants he pushes his hand down the opening of her dress, just at the crack of her buttocks. She thrusts them out in his hand.

One night Lulu dreamt of Tillie, the bag lady. She looked like Myra Schneider fallen on hard times.

Julian once told her Myra Schneider had had a Mongolian son. Nobody had ever seen him, but people knew about it.

. . .

189

They finally arrived at a camp, deep in the bushes, on the other side of the pass. It was set up around an abandoned shepherd's cabin. A few men, some in unmatched army gear, others in peasant clothes, were sitting with their backs to the cabin protected from the *mistral*, fanning a small fire above which hung a pot of coffee. The fire was kept low in order not to attract attention from a distance. David was greeted warmly. One man got up to hug him, calling him *camarade*. She stayed a little while, lingering next to him. He grew nervous and took her to the other side of the cabin where he pressed her passionately against him, running his tongue over her lips, touching her breasts, her crotch. She started unbuttoning his fly. He jumped back, you're crazy, he whispered. Any one of them could walk around, see what we're doing. Don't worry, she said. They wouldn't disturb lovers saying good-bye to each other. She opened the fly and pushed his underwear down and kneeled in front of him in the dark and sucked until he came in her mouth, swallowing every drop of him to remember his taste. I'll never love anyone else, she swore, sealing her vow with her lips.

When she reached the foot of the mountain the *mistral* was blowing at full force, hissing through the olive trees. She turned around before crossing the vineyard and saw the moon was red. Not red as it sometimes is at sunset. Red at midnight, high in the sky. The tops of the hills were in flames, reddening the horizon from which rose a scarlet smoke. She heard the sirens of the little fire trucks, she saw them driving down from the village, a long red caterpillar stretching along the valley road.

In the morning the smoke spread in the sky like a fog, then at noon the fire picked up again in two different areas, a little more to the east, pushed by the wind. On the radio evening news she heard five men had died, three of them firemen who burned up in their truck as the wind turned around. In the village they said that it was no accident, somebody had set the fire up in the hills.

Lulu touches her round breasts, holds them with her hands the way she liked Julian to hold them. Weighing them. Letting them hang heavily in her palms.

She searches her body, feels it. Looks at it with surprise. It doesn't belong to her. Nature is borrowing it from her as a receptacle to process its young, as she pleases. Each year, if she let nature have her way.

Lulu is walking, round belly, round breasts, long legs. She paces the streets, her eyes blind, her mind lost.

Lulu, Lucy, Lucilia, luminary, Ludovic. Lucidity. Luce. Luz, lux, Luxor, luxury. Luminous, luminosity. Lucifer, lunacy, lunatic, lunar. Lush, lust. Lullaby. Lurid. Ludicrous. Loony lunacy. Lulu's luminous on lunatic nights. Cool-hand Luke. Cool-hand Lulu. Lucky Luke. Lucky Lulu.

New York's heat, in summer, is not at all like the heat in the south of France. It's humid, subtropical. It never lets up. Night and day the fans swirl, the air-conditioners drip on the sidewalks. It drips on your neck like pigeon shit if you walk too close to the walls, which is not Lulu's case. Anyway this neighborhood is too poor for air-conditioning. People here set up little round fans perched on a table or a dresser, turning at high speed, ripping kids' fingers to mincemeat if they're not careful. Lulu loves the hot humid heat, she finds it sensual. She's already walked three times around the square full of chirping kids, pushers and winos, without paying them any attention, nor to the young artists dressed as low-life punks, their hair slashed with a nasty razor-blade, nor to the groups of young executives, guided by a real estate agent, appraising a burned-down tenement building with greedy eyes. She doesn't see any of this. She keeps walking around the park, staring at her feet, sweaty and dusty in their sandals. At the end of her fourth lap she turns on Eighth Street as if she had finally reached a decision. She walks fast, looking in front of her now.

The quartz is warm in her hand. It links her with something immaterial. The thread is so thin. It keeps breaking.

In the village they said the *maquisards* were caught in the fire. They found two bodies completely charred at the camp, but no trace of the other men. She listened to the rumors, holding her womb. When the smoke blew away, the hilltops over Pennafort were bald, spiked with stumps of blackened wood. The sky was pure, cleansed by the *mistral*.

Two windows are wide open on the mountains covered with pines. Lying down on the white piqué bedspread, she hears the tireless crickets, she sees the blue sky and, if she sits up, the ocher farmhouses with a few cypress trees clustered at the edge of the vineyards. She would never know if one of the bodies was his. Charred beyond recognition, people whispered in the street. The heat pours down on her stomach.

She is a carnival goddess, all dressed in gold. Vermeil skin, platinum nails, copper hair. She is a metal woman who sparkles in the sun. She is an armor woman who springs out of the earth, who dances and bounces, setting the glass city on fire with the heat borne of her mirrored reflections. She performs the dance of dawn on the river shores, her golden cuirass beating like cymbals before the rising sun.

I ask her what to do but I can't hear her voice. She keeps dancing in the sun.

Bodies have been loaded on a train, Lulu doesn't know if they are dead or alive. They are lying on stretchers, covered with sheets. Staff people push the stretchers inside the compartments, which they close with thick curtains. The sounds are muffled. Everyone speaks in low voices. Lulu goes from one compartment to another. They won't let her in. She pleads. Once or twice they let her peek or if they don't pay attention to her she sneaks in. She lifts blankets, studies faces. They don't look like corpses. She doesn't know what she's looking for. Yes, that's it. She's trying to recognize faces. They told her who to look for. She is a spy. It is war. These people are people they hide. Most of them are alive. She looks for cues, for marks. Nobody must know that these people are here. Top Secret. She looks around feverishly. She doesn't know whether she recognizes them. They all seem asleep. She mentally photographs the faces. The search goes on until she wakes up.

. . .

Lulu fell asleep three seconds after the shot and they took this life from her. She asked them to uproot the germ that had clung to her without her asking for it. And now she mourns it. She can't leave the deep seas. They haunt her.

My grandfather used to sing songs to me that my family called dirty songs: *Perrine était servan-te, Perrine était servan-te, ti-la-la-la dondain-ne.* I don't remember why it was supposed to be dirty. It was about a bidet, I think that's what it was. But I only remember the first line: *Perrine was a servant-girl, Perrine was a servant-girl* . . . My grandfather didn't go to Mass anymore, they didn't think that was good either. He said he was pantheist, that he believed in the presence of gods in nature. He thought he was deeply religious, more than those hypocrites who went to Mass every Sunday and sinned all the other days.

She came back empty-bellied. She came back curetted clean. She thought she would make a fresh start. When she woke up in the small aseptic room, grey metal, white tiles, curled up on her side, she felt the thick pad squeezed between her thighs. She pulled it out, she looked at the dried blood, brown, she sniffed at it. It didn't smell like period blood. It had a sweet smell of entrails.

The mint syrup she drinks at the café is synthetic emerald green in the faceted glass. She's passed through the eye of the needle and she's been turned inside out. The waiter with the Art of Loving T-shirt fills up filters with ground coffee under a fan. The edges of the stacked-up filters curl in the stirred air. At 8:25 A.M. they pushed her on the wheel-on stretcher and the doors from the hallway to the OR swung open. She was already under Valium. She was flying. She didn't jump from the table, she didn't scream.

Your personal ambition isn't worth a life, Mario said.

Of course. Of course.

Your personal ambition isn't worth a life.

Of course.

She fell asleep in three seconds after being hit by the IV.

. . .

My aunt and I are standing face to face in her Paris apartment. We raise our voices. I can't stand this life anymore, she says. I am torn apart.

I am going to attack her one more time. She goes on. I am going to kill myself. I want to get it over with.

I grab her by the throat, I want to press hard, real hard, I want to smother the voice in her throat. But I just push her away.

What do you know about being torn apart. You flourish your wounds as threats. You use your wounds for blackmail. But what about her. Wasn't she torn too? And me? It goes way back. I wouldn't be had by maternity. Me, the sagging-breasted hysterical *Hausfrau,* a litter of kids hanging from her apron! Or even the full-blown mother, a bit languid, pure complexion, ripe flesh!

I am a fatalist, Mario said. If I was a woman I would let nature run its course.

Sure. Fatalist like Muslim women locked up in their harem. Performing the millennium-old gestures, squatting, kneading the couscous in their palms rusted with henna, thrusting the pelvis forward, pushing the baby out. Life which comes out, blossoms, withers. Which gives its last breath away. Breathe, breathe, the midwife says. Now start panting. Go with the waves. Always the waves. Those pull your entrails apart. You surf on your belly. You go up the wave. Ride it. Okay now, breathe. Breathe deeply between contractions. During the lulls.

There was a storm of the devil. You could see like in full daylight at each flash of lightning. My mother went out silently and hailed a cab. It was the usual Paris under the rain. The shiny cobblestones, the cabs honking their horns, the race to get to the theater without being drenched. The feature. What was it? A Gabin maybe. Yes, *Quai des Brumes*. Yes, she must have liked Gabin. It was still raining and Paris smelled good after the film. She slowly walked toward Odéon. She had to sit on a wet bench across from the Luxembourg Gardens because her back hurt. Her belly was getting big and she stayed under the rain stroking it and looking at the car headlights run red and yellow on the asphalt until she was soaked.

It is one of these midsummer days with a bright sky that makes you think of the fall, back to school, wool sweaters, knee-high socks, renewed energy. But Lulu thinks blood. Blood dripping from her womb. She is clutched around her center, while the ivy on the wall across from her window ripples under the sea breeze. I am sinking. I am emptying myself. Full or empty, our alternative. Never opaque. Always this transparent space, this hole to fill or not, this potential, this availability.

New York thrusts her skyscrapers' needles like diamonds glimmering at her fingertips in the noon sun. The skirts flutter around women's hips at the corner of the long midtown canyons.

When I was a little girl my grandfather sang to me, *Perrine était servan-te, Perrine était servan-te, tra-la-la-li-dondain-ne.*

The clinic was surrounded by a garden full of flowers. It was a big villa with the birth rooms on the first floor. There were freshly cut roses in a glass vase in front of the window. Yellow and cream, their heads heavy. My mother wondered if the flowers would hold until the birth, which she imagined after a long tunnel of hours. The sheets were smooth with starch, the edge glossy under her fingers. There was no delivery room. The two midwives went from room to room. It was rare to have two women exactly at the same stage of labor. She heard moans muffled by the thick partitions, the gay voices of the midwives and the nurses when the doors opened, the wailing of a newborn baby. Her contractions were still well apart and manageable. They rolled through her belly at regular intervals.

Okay, you swell, you grow like a plant, you grow buds. You're not one but multiple. Nature grows through you, pushes you aside. Open up and let me drop this egg. Well. Lulu had refused to multiply herself like Jesus' rolls. She believed in the uniqueness of a human being. She believed she was finished, that she stopped at her fingernails and the ends of her hair. An accomplished human being, freshly cut and set in a vase. The idea to perpetuate oneself, to unfold oneself . . . It made her think of rabbits.

There were four of them in the foyer. Two had come with their men, who were politely asked to leave. Lulu was alone. They didn't look at one another. They were sent to the elevator, then dispatched to different bedrooms for the trimmings: undressing, blood test, Valium shot. They were back together eight hours later downstairs, minus the foetuses, their purses slung on their shoulders as after a day's work, their hair freshly combed, just a shade paler, and courteously held the door for one another before vanishing into the rush-hour crowd.

Okay now, stop panting. Breathe deeply. Good. Breathe again. The midwife said she was nine centimeters dilated. It was a day and a night and many hours after her arrival at the clinic. The contractions came so fast she couldn't keep up with her breathing, she felt like a broken ship tossed over and over against a cliff but her hand squeezed the midwife's hand and she hung on to her words as if they were incantations, her whole being concentrated on the sound of that voice, on the pressure of that hand in hers. Then all of a sudden everything quieted down. She propped herself on one elbow and announced she had to go to the bathroom. The midwife said no, it meant the time had come. Wait, don't push yet. The midwife positioned herself between her legs, a nurse held her back and she was told to push. She pushed so hard she thought her inner ears would explode. She pushed and she pushed but the head—my head—still wasn't coming out. They introduced the forceps in her cunt. She moaned. It was a cold pain, an artificial stretch that forced the muscles open. The metal prongs spooned me up and pulled but something wasn't working out. Maybe my shoulders didn't present themselves properly. The pain was atrocious. I resisted it, trying to reach back inside, caught between the two worlds. Her sister appeared next to her. She said, the child will never make it, we can't take that chance. The midwife said everything was okay. It would just take some time. Let her rest for a few minutes. She was tired after the long labor. It was normal. Her pushing was not efficient. In a case like that it just takes a little longer. My aunt started to raise her voice. She said she was going to call an ambulance, that it was a crime, she wanted my mother to be sent to a hospital, it was obvious they had to do a Caesarean section. The midwives asked my aunt to leave the room, they told her firmly that they were in charge, they knew what they were doing. Finally I came out screaming, gasping. My head was shaped like a football, elongated by the forceps. My mother fainted out of exhaustion. They put me on the bottle right away. I looked for something that wasn't there. Something warm and soft. An outside corresponding to the inside.

During the
Olympic Games

The words LOS ANGELES 1984 XXIIIRD OLYMPIAD blaze on
the screen. It's hot over there, they tell you. Eighty-five, ninety
degrees, you get to know the temperature in L.A. better than in
New York. The sunset is postcard perfect, dripping gold on a
Pacific so calm it's hard to imagine it swelling into surf. The
runners stagger, drunk with heat, fatigue. They collapse under
the glaring sun. They bite the dust. Spread out belly down. Mario,
as far as he is concerned, is cool, in his little room at the back
of the bar, with a fan blowing directly on his face.

Mario is lying on his bed, bare feet sticking out of his jeans,
shoulders propped up by a pillow. The tv remote-control is sitting
on his belly, as if wired to it. In his right hand a strawberry ice
cream float is turning beige. He seems frozen in a slight catatonic
state. Only his fingers show any sign of life, as they move at
intervals to press the buttons from channel to channel.

A beautiful black man, his legs two ebony pillars, his lips sensual, his eyes on fire. He runs his fingers through his short cropped hair. Squatting, he puts one foot against the starting block. Ready, get set, GO!!! Scrambling sneakered feet and black calves on the track.

Julian arrives at Lulu's place holding a bouquet of flowers. He says he ran into Mystique in the street and she told him what happened. Lulu doesn't know whether she is happy to see him or not. Since her abortion she is feeling out of touch. And anyway she is watching the Olympic Games. She makes room for him on the couch next to her.

A blond, extremely blond man stands on a high platform, his magnificent body stretched in the sun. His toes, only his toes, hug the side of what looks now like a trampoline. He springs lightly up and down as if moved by a soft breeze. In spite of the fact that this man must weigh at least 180 pounds, his whole body rests, perfectly relaxed, at the edge of a ten-foot-high springboard, on the strength of ten little toes.

Lulu gets up to mix some iced coffee in the kitchen.

The man goes up without a bang. He flies. Tilts. His whole body, taut, a baton twirling up in the air, twists three times, tucks itself in, legs folded tight in the arms, turns again three times, then stretches out and knifes the silky skin of the water without a splash.

Jesus! Did you see that?

In L.A. it rains gold medals on American athletes crying for joy. Among the crowd, lovingly panned by an ABC-TV camera, Dustin Hoffman blinks behind his metal-rimmed round sunglasses. His hair is cropped tight against his skull. In profile his nose is like a beak, his lips a thin line.

It's a hot and dusty afternoon when Mystique flies in from her mother's funeral in Dayton, Ohio, overwhelmed by the clamor outside Port Authority. Street vendors are pushing their wares, a group of kids just out of school in summer uniforms, green gabardine shorts or pleated skirts and white shirts, are pursuing each other and yanking their packs off each other's shoulder blades, yelling insults like stupid ass and noisily popping bubble gum as Mystique elbows her way through their little crowd. The smell of New York—overripe garbage and gasoline—catches her at the throat, and for the first time since her mother's died she stops feeling like crying. She is stunned. Anaesthetized. She thinks of calling Lulu, to make contact with life, pull herself back into this world. Her mother's death belongs to nature, like birth, fires, earthquakes, tidal waves, forces that are stronger than us, make us feel out of control, sweep us out of ourselves. New York is completely out of control, but of a particular, synthetic out-of-control kind. Like control gone berserk. As if the more you try to deny nature's forces the more they make their way back into this artificial, man-made world, but in a perverted way.

She doesn't call Lulu. With her she would have tried to numb herself of the fear. She has used up her tears. What she feels now isn't pain or loss. It is the utter solitude, sense of oneness. The blunt, crude blow of it slamming her in the face. Then she wonders, and immediately feels guilty about it, am I going to start living now? Did I hide behind her all my life? Did I use her as a shield? Mystique decides not to go home. This hot rathole seething with clothes crammed in plastic bags and cat food spilling out of dishes she calls home.

Instead she proceeds, calmly, to canvas the streets of Midtown, working her way south and east alternatively, from one avenue to another via slightly cooler side streets, forcing herself into a rhythm that makes sweat ooze at her armpits and around her hairline and nape. She gets whiffs of her own smell from time to time and tries to hang onto it as a reassurance of her own existence.

The news fades into a stupid game with blond women flashing lots of teeth and waving overgrown garishly painted fingernails toward the camera. Mario turns off the tv with a sigh, draining whatever remains of his strawberry float, tepid and watery. He gets up, splashes water on his hair and gets ready to leave his room.

Julian is lying down on the couch, his head on Lulu's lap. His hair's growing back into its natural color, reddish blond, but the tips are still jet black. Lulu runs her fingers through it. His body feels light on her, angular, after Mario's rounder flesh. On Lulu's marble mantel sits a wedding invitation engraved in thick off-white parchment, with a hand-written note signed Henry that says, dear Lulu, I'll love you always. I wish you the best . . . Lulu feels light, light as if nothing mattered anymore. She strokes Julian's hair and follows the line of his chin, of his lips with her fingers.

It's a hot summer night. People are playing their boxes loud in the street. *Salsa* and rap beats rise up to the open windows, mixing with the soft swirling of the fan blades. The minister of the church next door is yelling in his microphone from the backyard. He screams JUNKIES! SAVE YOURSELVES! at the top of his lungs and they laugh together. Julian raises his arm toward her. His skin is white and transparent. Even in summer with the sun, he never seems to get a tan. Their arms meet, stretch against each other, entwine. He pops the snap of her jeans, pulls the zipper down, peels off the pants down to her legs, kneels before her. His tongue along her thighs again, the touch of his hands again wake up nerve endings she thought had become numb. She pushes her hands under his T-shirt, she wants to feel his strange white flesh. She feels the bruised lines along his back, follows the thin scars with her fingers. She pulls him to her, she sighs to the touch that troubles her. COME BACK TO GOD screams the minister, and they laugh again. Lulu rolls her T-shirt up above her breasts, massaging them in her hands till the nipples stand erect and tender while her sex drips in Julian's mouth.

Mario is on his way to Lulu's place. He climbs the narrow staircase, running up to the fifth floor. He turns the key into the lock, since he came back from Mexico he's kept the key, he didn't bother to call, he was in the neighborhood, he thought he'd just stop by, see what she was up to.

They don't hear the key, the noise from the street is pretty intense, a group of people getting a barbecue ready in the vacant lot across the street or maybe the minister's speech has reached a high-pitched climax, in any case, Mario is already standing in the doorway when Lulu becomes aware of a presence and lifts her eyes. She makes a move or maybe utters a slight muffled exclamation that alerts Julian, he turns around, registers Mario's frame by the door, and proceeds to wipe his mouth glistening with Lulu's cum with the side of his arm then slowly gets up while she quietly stares at Mario without attempting to pull her clothes together. Mario sees Julian's cool composure and Lulu's provocative nonchalance and a total lack of denial on their part of what's going on and he flips out. He drops the paper bag holding a six-pack he's been carrying and marches on Julian, grabbing him by the throat. He says motherfucker, motherfucker several times, yanking his T-shirt around his neck so hard it rips in half down his chest. Julian tries to protect himself with his forearms. Lulu manages to squeeze between them, holding Mario by the wrists. She says, this is between you and me, leave him out of this. Mario gives her a kick on the shin that propels her on the couch. She springs back and yells, I am not a prize that you guys are going to fight for. If you're pissed Mario let *me* have it. Who I am sleeping with is *my* business. Mario cringes. Julian says, you're nuts, man, you're nuts and tries to elbow his way out of Mario's hands, edging toward the wall. And suddenly Mario pulls his blade out.

He's got his knees flexed, his elbows loose at the waist, he's bouncing from foot to foot, his left arm ready to dodge an attack. But there's no attack, Julian steps back, raises his hands. He says, hey man, cool it man. Lulu tells Mario to put his blade down, she's going to call the cops. Mario keeps bouncing forward, saying you're gonna get it man. Lulu says, let me explain. Put it down, I want to talk to you. Mario! Julian's hands are completely raised now in surrender, he backs off against the couch. Mario says, I'm listening. Go ahead. What do you have to say for yourself? Still juggling with the switchblade, still moving on Julian. Lulu says, I won't talk if you don't put that fucking blade down. Then she says she's known Julian for a long time, before she even met Mario. Mario looks at her, waiting for more. Lulu says he just stopped by and then . . . Mario waits. Lulu says, things haven't been so good between us since Mexico, right? Mario: whose fault is it? Lulu says she's been upset, she needs time to think, she never promised him . . . Put it DOWN Mario! Mario: who's this asshole who was sucking you? Isn't he the little fag who was putting makeup on one day backstage at the Blue Night Lounge? Can't even fuck you, right? Can't get it up for a woman, *maricón!* Lulu says fuck you Mario. Julian's lips are curling up in a wicked sneer. Mario lowers his hand and folds the blade in, his eyes on Lulu. He now completely ignores Julian. He says, man, you almost had my baby. And all this time you were seeing this faggot. There was no baby, Lulu says. I was pregnant. It had nothing to do with you.

Julian is tucking his T-shirt back in his pants, the two ripped parts flapping on his chest. He says, okay, I'm splitting. It was nice talking to you guys. Mario spits on the floor behind his back. Julian doesn't turn around. They watch him leave in silence.

After they hear the front door bang, Mario turns to Lulu who's stretched on the couch, her legs on the coffee table, too relaxed looking for his taste.

Now listen, bitch, he says. Don't fuck with me.

After the
hurricane

The cat is curled up on Lulu's kitchen table, one foot on her book, his soft orange ears quivering at intervals as if a quick dream was running through his sleep. The New York Mutual Life Insurance Building pyramid top is shimmering like gold lamé. The hurricane has passed, sweeping the sky to a radiant blue, leaving behind a hearty sea wind still busy in the leaves and branches of the trees. The city was expecting powerful forces uprooting trees, shaking windows, knocking down awnings, flooding streets, 130 mph gusts of wind leaving citizens foolish enough to stay out in the streets gasping, ten-foot waves sweeping across South Ferry, all bridges closed, the FDR and the Westside Highway flooded, the World Trade Center dangerously swaying in the storm. But other than heavy rains pouring out of an ominous black sky all morning, Manhattan remained quiet. The great twirling storm unexpectedly slowed down above the mid-

Atlantic's cooler waters and meekly broke against Long Island's south shore, causing some banal several million dollars damage that probably didn't necessitate the evacuation of half a million people. Millions more, off from work, waited all morning glued to their tv sets, tension mounting, for the steady rain to pick up and for the winds to hit. What a joke, Lulu thinks, watching the sky now innocently clear, before turning on her answering machine and stuffing her keys in her backpack, my windows didn't even rattle.

Mario is waiting for her at the foot of the steps, his back against the linden tree shedding its leaves in the wind. He's kicking a piece of cement around with the tip of his basketball sneaker. He looks mean and stubborn, like a not-too-smart kid who's only got one idea in his head, and not a good one at that. Lulu plays it matter-of-fact. What's up Mar? she asks. He repeats, what's up Mar? resorting to infantile and irritating tactics. She tells him she's on her way to the subway and does he want to walk with her? He says, damn right! After which she prudently shuts up and they walk side by side, him forcing his stride down to accommodate her slower pace. His energy feels brittle and dangerous like broken glass splintered underfoot. For a long time they don't talk, until they get to Astor Place and he kicks the huge black cube poised in the middle of the island at the center, making it swing on its edge.

She says, hey, what's the matter? He says shit and that she treats him like some kinda stud. She starts to shake violently like when she had been caught with a puddle of pee dripping from her seat in fourth grade because she hadn't dared ask to go to the toilet during class. Guilt flushes her face all the way to her neck and spreads burning through her whole body. He doesn't have to tell her. She knows: she's not faithful to him, she's seen Julian again, she uses him sexually, she's embarrassed to introduce him to her friends because he's Puerto Rican and he's from the street. What else? She's a fucking racist. She says, don't tell me. I know all the fucking stereotypes about me and you. He says, what do you know! and proceeds to tell her what's wrong with her. They're standing on the corner by the subway entrance at Broadway and Eighth Street where the ChemBank wall juts out. People streaming out of the subway keep saying excuse me, excuse me as they block part of the passage. She says let's go somewhere else, but Mario's got her locked against the wall within his arms and she doesn't really mean to get out. She's busy defending herself.

His rage vibrates against her chest. He spills his heart in vicious spirals that reach deep. His anger is not rejecting. It's a plea for approval, for love. All I'd have to do, she thinks, is to put my arms around his waist, between the ruggedness of the Levi's jacket and the heavily belted jeans, in the soft chink of the armor, on the T-shirt thin and vulnerable like skin, run my hands along the ribcage. This would be a good place for a passionate kiss. He would unleash his passion, twirl his tongue around mine, an invisible sexual ballet performed in full daylight in the middle of a crowd. He would press his sex against me, jam one knee between my legs, knowing exactly where I need it. I'd squeeze my hands under his pants and feel the tautness of his ass, run a finger down the crack.

But she doesn't touch him. She watches his fists pound the wall. His hands betray him, coarse skin, sores, cuts, thick nails grown longer than men usually do, dirt encased in the pores, hands skillful at tuning a guitar, beating a drum, rolling a joint, changing a tire, but uncomfortable with a pen or a demitasse. His hands are where her class prejudices, in this instant, concentrate in a lethal dose. As they spread next to her or curl up in fists she reads ignorance and peasant heritage and unfinished high school. Where she comes from they're all fucked in the head but they have delicate pale racy hands revealing work of the mind and help in the kitchen. She knows them well, his hands. They've touched the inside of her thighs. They've traced lines around her lips. Their ruggedness on her breasts made her moan. She watched them hold a fork like a weapon, stabbing the meat and nailing it perpendicular to the plate, looking at them with the same sense of foreignness as if they had been maneuvering chopsticks. Now she watches them pound the wall. They're live pain with their sores and bruises. They're live poverty and she doesn't want to look at them. His anger spent, he rests his back against the wall.

The wind blows nastily up Broadway, as if sucked into a funnel, and hits the corner where they're standing in sharp gusts smelling of sea. They stay speechless for a while, side by side.

I got to go, she says finally. I got things to do.

So is that it?

I don't *know*.

She holds him by the shoulders, she squeezes them desperately. His soul seems to have flown out of him with his anger. He is hard and tight and about as alive as a slab of cement. She feels like she's holding on to a pair of dungareed shoulders.

I'll talk to you, she says.

The last
chapter

Mario is kneeling near his bedside table in a dim light, moving candles around, scribbling geometric figures entwined with letters on scraps of paper. With the help of an X-acto he engraves the sides of a black candle with the same signs he has designed on paper. He lights the candle and sets it with dripping wax on a saucer, then squats in front of it, his eyes staring at the short flickering flame till he loses his consciousness in the moving light rising from the wick.

It is Sunday afternoon, the crowd walks the alleys of Tompkins Square Park, groups of skinheads in heavy leather boots in spite of the weather, old Ukrainians in clusters playing chess on the stone tables or warming up their faces to the sun, eyes half-closed, a cane between their legs. The Poet has set himself up on the bandshell. His box is at his feet, blaring louder than usual, a red tie impeccably knotted under his jacket, his arms crossed over his chest. He's closed his eyes and he listens to his monologue, whispering it to himself. It's about God and about a child who doesn't want her parents to watch tv and presses stick-ons on the screen to cover the announcer's head, and about a cop who had fifty-two decorations and was charged with sexually abusing his eight-year-old daughter fifty-two times and two old ladies with blue hair who owned a sandwich shop in southern Florida called Chubby Chicken and Honey Bunny, and had skin hanging from their chins and cameos pinned at the collar of their blouses and who were raped one night in their apartment at the back of the shop and at the trial the judge said the accused was drunk and jumped into the sack with them, had sex and went to sleep and the judge said that it started without consent maybe but he thought the old ladies ended up enjoying themselves.

Julian walks into the bar. It's virtually empty in the afternoon, except for a few hangers-on scattered at tables or arguing with each other or a band setting up for the evening. The bar usually only comes alive way into the night, after the regular customers have left and the legal places have closed, when the hard-core night crowd shows up for a nightcap. He has a few words with the bartender. He's looking for dope. The usual sources seem to have dried up for the moment. The bartender motions to the door at the back. Julian knocks and walks in. Mario's candle is burning behind a small screen, Julian's eyes are briefly attracted to the light and the shadow of the flame rising above the screen on the wall, then he sees Mario and stops dead in his tracks. Mario's eyes are hard and suspicious. Julian nods to him, he says I think we've met before. Mario says, what the fuck do you want?

The sidewalk is covered with discarded furniture, an old fridge with the door ripped off, a disemboweled tv set, dressers with gaping holes in place of drawers, a mattress propped against the garbage cans. But what you notice the most is plastic bags all over the place, huge trash bags on their sides like some old wounded dogs getting ready to die, bags gorged with clothes spilling out on rusted kitchen appliances, an old two-door toaster, utensils piled in a cabinet drawer, a couple of aluminum pots bottom up. Piles of old *Life* magazines have toppled between the bags and a whole record collection has been kicked and splinters of black vinyl lie in the middle of the sidewalk just where people will step on them.

The first-floor window, the one a little below ground level, is all boarded up behind stars of broken glass. The front door is boarded up. The lower windows are sealed with cinderblocks. The others are black empty holes without glass. The whole place is empty. All the squatters have been evicted. Now a large pipe hangs from a top window toward a hypothetical dumpster, unmistakable sign of renovation.

You remember the bag lady with the little felt hat who used to lounge around that old couch on Avenue B? Lulu asks Mystique as they walk past the building. She used to live here.

I know, Mystique says. Tillie.

She's dead. When the new landlord took over the building they came to exterminate her place while she was there, lying in bed. She was too sick to leave, I think she had pneumonia or something, so they sprayed with her still in the apartment and they exterminated her along with the roaches. Afterwards they threw out all her stuff on the sidewalk, just like that. She was the only tenant left in the whole place. The building is supposed to become a luxury co-op.

RAPHAEL DEVITO'S LATEST FILM A LETDOWN

The name catches Lulu's eye in a bookstore where she is leafing through magazines and newspapers. It's a review of Raphael's new movie. Her eyes scan rapidly through the names of the actors and the details of the story line to get to the meat of the matter:

Raphael DeVito's first features' verve and high energy have turned into a shallow and pretentious, self-referential and self-congratulatory exercise which is all style and no content and cannot be redeemed by a weak, convoluted and ultimately badly plotted story and wooden acting.

A smile breaks on Lulu's face. She knew it would happen sooner or later. She's worked so hard at it, using Mario's technique with the candles. She buys the newspaper and hurries home to clip the article, rereads it with satisfaction, folds it neatly and puts it away in a folder.

She dreams about Myra Schneider. Myra Schneider is dressed all in black. She looks much older. Her high cheekbones, so insolent when she was a younger woman, rise like unsubmerged islets out of the collapse of her sunken cheeks. The eyes have deepened in their sockets, have turned a washed-out grey-blue, milky like those of a newborn babe whose eye color has not yet settled. She doesn't dance any more with the handsome officer who used to hold her tight against him, she squeezes a cane against her sore hip. She wears long skirts and black curate's laced-up boots. She has forgotten the names of her lovers and only remembers that of her Mongolian son, who died at twenty-seven in an institution for the mentally handicapped. The baby, she asks her nurse. Is he still asleep? It's not true that he is Mongolian, she says. He has the eyes of his grandfather, who had Japanese blood.

At 8:30 A.M. Lulu gets a call from Salvine who tells her Julian OD'ed the night before. He was spending the evening in some guy's apartment and the guy called the ambulance. The only address they found on him was Salvine's and she was notified in the middle of the night. She says to Lulu, I knew you two were very close. Does Lulu hear a note of jealousy in her voice? Salvine goes on, I thought you'd want to know right away. Her voice is controlled. It's low, firm, somewhat detached. She says, it didn't hit me yet. Lulu's stunned. It's early for her, she worked at the club the night before and didn't come home till late. She stares at the Japanese shades that turn the sunlight into a glowing white. Oh no oh no she repeats.

I always thought he would die like that, Salvine says, that he was always pushing it. Always at the edge . . . You know how he always carried that stupid switchblade, how he'd hang out in the park late at night?

Who was the guy he was with? Lulu asks.

I don't know. Someone he picked up last night. He didn't even know Julian's last name. He knew nothing about him.